Dedicated to my three nuts:

Kyra, Lea, and Mallory.

You make my heart smile.

-Stephanie Sorkin

The author's proceeds from the sale of this book will be donated to FARE, dedicated to food allergy research and education.

Nutley, the Nut-Free Squirrel

Story © 2013 by Stephanie Sorkin

PRT0213A

Printed in the United States

ISBN-13: 9781620861585
ISBN-10: 1620861585

Library of Congress Control Number: 2012950726

www.mascotbooks.com

NUTLEY

the Nut-Free Squirrel

Stephanie Sorkin

Illustrated by Tim Warren

Hello! My name is Nutley.
I know this may sound strange,
but I'm a nut-free squirrel.
I guess I should explain.

See, one day I was feeling starved.

My belly growled so...

I reached for what a squirrel eats.

At the time, I did not know...

That nuts were not okay for me
to eat like most squirrels do.
My eyes puffed up!
Some hives popped out!
An allergy, it's true.

After all the itching stopped,
I knew I'd need a plan
so that this would not happen
again,
and again,
and again.

So I called a meeting in a tree
for my pals from far and near.
They all showed up to find out how
to help a friend so dear.

Surprising as it is to all,
since I do live in a tree,
I must avoid peanuts and tree nuts
to keep myself healthy.

My doctor said to play it safe;
avoidance is best.
And once a year, or sometimes twice,
I'll have to take a test.

A squirrel allergic to nuts—how odd!
I thought I'd feel alone
'til one of my friends stood up
and declared,
"I'm a dog allergic to bones!"

"I know just how you feel," said the fly,
a little voice so cute.
"I have a similar problem
only mine's with pitted fruit."

"My problems," said the bee, "are the trees that bloom.
The pollen makes me sneeze.
I rub my wings and scratch my back
after even the slightest breeze."

"I hope you all can hear me," said the pelican.
"My voice is very low.
I cannot eat the fish that swim
in the water down below."

"Wow! I can't believe my ears!" shouted Nutley.
"Some others have allergies, too!
We'll have to keep each other safe
like buddies always do."

We went around the group real slow
and spoke one at a time.
We all talked about our favorite treats.
Gummi bears are mine.

Now, my friends bring nut-free sweets.
They really do not mind.
I know they love me more and more
cause I'm one of a kind.

Turn the page
for a delicious...
nutritious...
nut-free
recipe!

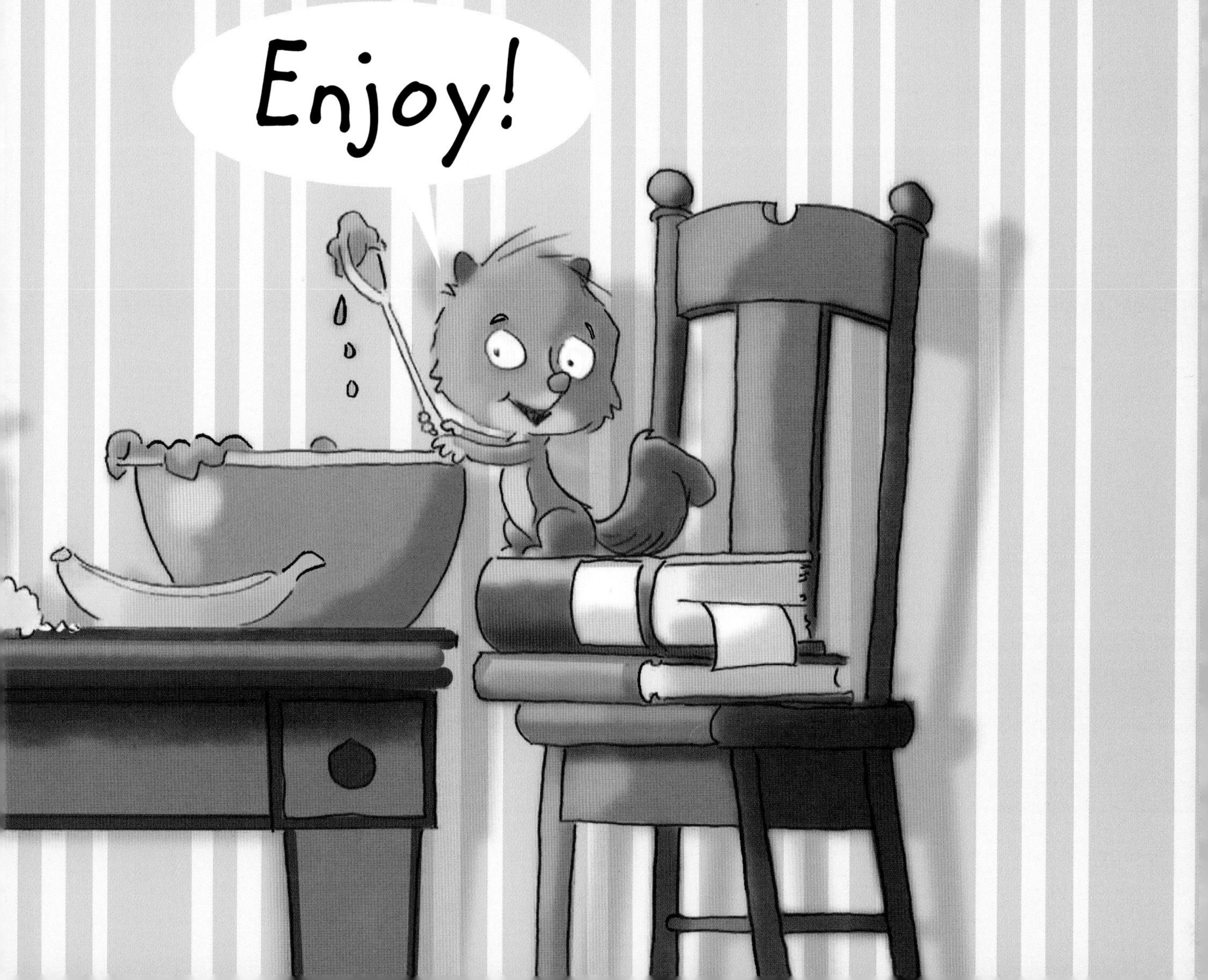

Yummy Nut-Free Banana Bread

Ingredients

- 1/2 cup (1 stick) butter (soft or slightly melted)
- 6 ounces Greek yogurt
- 1 1/2 cups sugar
- 2 1/2 cups flour
- 3-4 medium, ripe bananas
- 1 teaspoon vanilla extract
- 1 teaspoon baking soda
- 1 teaspoon salt

Did I mention it's egg-free, too?

Directions

- Preheat oven to 350 degrees.

- Grease the bottom only of the loaf pan.

- In a mixer, mix butter and sugar. Add Greek yogurt, mashed bananas, and vanilla. Stir to combine.

- Add flour, baking soda, and salt. Consistency will be sticky and thick.

- Pour into loaf pan.

- Bake for 1 hour, but start testing with a toothpick after 45 minutes.

- Let cool for 30 minutes then carefully run a knife around the edges of the loaf pan to loosen up the bread.

- Turn the pan over to remove bread and let cool on a plate.

This recipe can easily be made dairy-free and/or gluten-free! For dairy-free banana bread, replace the Greek yogurt with Tofutti brand non-dairy sour cream and replace the butter with parve margarine such as Fleischmann's or Mother's Brand. To make gluten-free banana bread, simply replace the regular flour with gluten-free rice flour.

Stephanie Sorkin lives in New York with her husband and three children. She is a member of The Society of Children's Book Writers and Illustrators. While Stephanie has written numerous children's books, she is extremely proud of *Nutley, the Nut-Free Squirrel* since all of the book proceeds will be donated to food allergy research and education.

CULTURES OF THE WORLD®

TAIWAN

Azra Moiz & Janice Wu

大中至正

MARSHALL **C**AVENDISH **B**ENCHMARK

NEW YORK

PICTURE CREDITS

Cover photo: © Porterfield-Chickering / Photo Researchers, Inc.

alt.TYPE / Reuters: 1, 5, 16, 34, 38, 48, 51, 53, 62, 81, 84, 108, 112, 118 • Audrius Tomonis (www.banknotes.com): 135 • Bes Stock: 26 • Far East Trade Service Inc.: 11, 88, 93 • Focus Team: 110, 124, 126 • HBL Network Photo Agency: 6, 40, 44, 45, 65, 86 • Hulton Deutsch: 29, 30, 67 • Hutchison Library: 3, 39, 42, 59, 69 • Life File Photos Ltd: 21, 94, 100 • Mark de Fraeye: 7, 10, 13, 15, 19, 22, 23, 25, 46, 54, 64, 66, 68, 70, 71, 72, 73, 74, 77, 78, 79, 80, 82, 90, 91, 96, 97, 99, 101, 106, 107, 113, 116, 117, 119, 122, 123, 125, 127, 128 • Photobank / Photolibrary Singapore: 14, 28, 36, 60, 63, 105, 120 • Taipei Representative Office: 4, 9, 18, 20, 85, 98, 103, 115 • The Image Bank: 47, 58, 75, 89

PRECEDING PAGE

Enthusiastic Taiwanese waving flags at the Chiang Kai-shek Memorial Hall.

Editorial Director (U.S.): Michelle Bisson
Editors: Deborah Grahame, Mabelle Yeo, Sharon Low
Copyreader: Daphne Hougham
Designers: Jailani Basari, Richard Lee
Cover picture researcher: Connie Gardner
Picture researchers: Thomas Khoo, Joshua Ang

Marshall Cavendish Benchmark
99 White Plains Road
Tarrytown, NY 10591
Web site: www.marshallcavendish.us

Originated and designed by Times Editions
An imprint of Marshall Cavendish International (Asia) Private Limited
A member of Times Publishing Limited

All Internet sites were correct and accurate at the time of printing. All monetary figures in this publication are in U.S. dollars.

Library of Congress Cataloging-in-Publication Data
Moiz, Azra, 1963–
    Taiwan / by Azra Moiz & Janice Wu.— 2nd. ed.
      p. cm. — (Cultures of the world)
    Audience: Ages 11+.
    Audience: Grades 7–8.
    Summary: "Provides comprehensive information on the geography, history, governmental structure, economy, cultural
      diversity, peoples, religion, and culture of Taiwan" — Provided by publisher.
    Includes bibliographical references and index.
      ISBN-13: 978-0-7614-2069-9
      ISBN-10: 0-7614-2069-X
    1. Taiwan—Juvenile literature. I. Wu, Janice. II. Title. III. Cultures of the world (2nd ed.)
    DS799.M65 2006
    951.24'9—dc22   2006002288

Printed in China

9 8 7 6 5 4 3 2 1

CONTENTS

Matsu Temple at Deer Ear Gate in T'ai-nan.

A game of diablo, in which the player, using the two sticks to tense the string, can toss the diablo into the air and catch it again.

INTRODUCTION

THE HISTORY OF THE REPUBLIC of China on Taiwan is closely linked with a number of Asian and European countries including China, Japan, Spain, Portugal, and the Netherlands. It was really only in the 20th century that Taiwan came into its own and forged a separate identity. It may be small, but it has achieved a degree of prosperity disproportionate to its size. In just four decades, it has made the leap from being a poor agricultural society to being one of Asia's most dynamic industrial economies. Taiwan's economic success and its problematic political standing in the international arena have often overshadowed the island's natural beauty as well as its multifaceted culture. Nevertheless, while the island's natural landscape presents stunning and dramatic geographical vistas—jagged mountains in the central region contrast with the flat wide plains in the coastal regions—it is the people of Taiwan who bear within them the essence of the island's nature. These are the very people whose heritage and traditions have spanned the centuries and who, despite political difficulties, face the future with confidence and conviction.

GEOGRAPHY

THE REPUBLIC OF CHINA ON Taiwan is an island nation that lies 100 miles (160 km) off the southeastern coast of mainland China, now the People's Republic of China (PRC). China is Taiwan's closest neighbor to the west. Korea and Japan lie to the north and the Philippines to the south. The Tropic of Cancer, which runs across the earth's surface at a latitude of 23.5°N, cuts across the island about midway.

Compared with its giant mainland neighbor, China, Taiwan is a small island with an area of 13,969 square miles (36,179 square km). This makes it slightly smaller than Switzerland or the Netherlands, or about the combined area of Connecticut, Massachusetts, and Rhode Island. The shape of the island has been likened to a tobacco leaf—it is long and tapers

Left: **The Taiwan Strait, also known as the Formosa Strait, separates Taiwan from China. It is approximately 100 miles (160 km) wide and is part of the South China Sea.**

Opposite: **The Central Mountain Range extends over much of Taiwan and is one of the island's top scenic attractions.**

at its southern end. At its broadest point, the island of Taiwan is 89 miles (144 km) wide; from north to south, it is 244 miles (394 km) long.

The Republic of China consists mostly of Taiwan but it also has jurisdiction over small groups of scattered islands. These include the Penghu archipelago with its 64 islands off the western coast of Taiwan, Kinmen (Quemoy) and Matsu islands, as well as 20 other islands, including Lü-tao (Green Island), Lan-yü (Orchid Island), and Chimei.

As Taiwan itself is an island, the seas are an important feature of its geography. The Taiwan Strait (or Formosa Strait) separates Taiwan from China to the west, and the Bashi Channel divides it from the Philippines to the south. To the north lies the East China Sea and to the east, the Pacific Ocean.

Taiwan is one of a chain of islands in the western Pacific. Over 10,000 years ago, during the last Ice Age when sea levels were lower, it is believed that Taiwan may have been connected to the mainland by a land bridge. Today, any land bridge is submerged under the Taiwan Strait, but the fact that sea depths in the strait are relatively shallow, about 230 feet (70 m) deep, has been used to support the theory behind the land bridge. In contrast, off the east coast of Taiwan, in the Pacific Ocean, the sea depth plummets to thousands of feet.

GEOGRAPHICAL REGIONS

Taiwan has one of the most varied landscapes in Asia, all within short distances of each other—snowcapped mountains and subtropical bamboo forests, sandy beaches and white-water rapids, gentle green hills and deep rocky gorges. Almost two-thirds of the island is covered with the mountains of the Central Range, and the rest is made up of foothills, terraced tablelands or plateaus, coastal plains, and basins. About 90 percent of Taiwan's

In the Central Mountain Range stands Taiwan's highest peak, Yü Shan. With so many high mountains and well-maintained mountain huts, there is no shortage of hiking trails.

population is located in the more low-lying areas of the terraced tablelands and coastal plains. Because 50 percent of the land is forested and almost 40 percent is used for agriculture and other purposes, approximately only 10 percent of it remains to house Taiwan's current population of 22.9 million people and to accommodate its industries.

CENTRAL MOUNTAIN RANGE AND OTHER MOUNTAINS Believed to have been formed over 1 million years ago by the collision of the earth's continental plates, the Central Mountain Range is Taiwan's most dominant physical feature. Stretching from Eluanbi in the south to Su-ao in the north, the long line of mountains rises gently in the west but plunges dramatically into the sea on the eastern coastline. More than 60 peaks in the Central Range soar above 10,000 feet (3,000 m). The highest mountain is Yü Shan (YOO-shahn), meaning Jade Mountain, in Yü Shan National Park.

Yü Shan is actually a large mountain mass made up of 11 peaks. Its main peak is the highest point in northeast Asia, standing at 12,965 feet (3,952 m). Along the eastern margin of the Central Range, the mountains rise steeply, creating spectacular scenery with deep gorges and valleys. A narrow coastal belt lies along the east coast where the mountains end.

To the west, the incline of the mountains is more gradual as they slope down gently into foothills and plains.

For many years, the mountainous Central Range posed a natural barrier to traveling to the isolated eastern regions. In 1960 the East-West Cross-Island Highway was constructed at a cost of $11 million. Built to facilitate travel within Taiwan, the highway stretches from the western coastal plain to the east coast, curving 120 miles (193 km) across the Central Mountains. This highway has helped to open up the eastern region to farming, cattle raising, logging, and tourism.

Taiwan also has pockets of volcanic mountains. The Tatun Mountains, located north of Taipei and near Chi-lung, are of volcanic origin. The presence of hot springs and fumaroles issuing hot gases shows that this northern region still has some geothermal activity. On the northeastern coast, some mountains of volcanic origin can also be found. Consequently, this area experiences frequent earthquakes and earth tremors.

Hot springs and sulfur pools, which are rich in minerals, are visible signs of ongoing geothermal activity.

FOOTHILLS AND TERRACED TABLELANDS Around the mountains of the Central Range lie the foothills. Most of the foothills are on the western side of the range, and they have an average height of 4,000–5,000 feet (1,220–1,520 m). Terraced tablelands—sandstone gravel deposits accumulated from erosion—lie between the foothills and coastal plains, at elevations of 330–1,640 feet (100–500 m). The broadest tableland can be found in the region between T'ao-yüan County and Hsin-chu County in northern Taiwan.

COASTAL PLAINS AND BASINS Coastal plains run along the western coast from the north to the southern tip of the island. Their rich and fertile alluvial soil has supported waves of immigrants from the mainland for hundreds of years, earning them the appellation "the rice bowl of Taiwan." The flat terrain of the western coast contrasts with the rugged mountains of the Central Range. As the plains are well drained by rivers, they are the focus of agriculture and settlement. The largest is the Chianan plain in the southwest, which makes up 12 percent of Taiwan's land area. Taiwan's major urban centers are located in the coastal basins—the Taipei Basin in the north, T'ai-chung

Much of Taiwan's rich variety of agricultural produce comes from the terraced land of the island's many plains and foothills.

Basin in the central west, and P'ing-tung Basin in the south. Three major municipalities—Taipei, T'ai-chung, and Kao-hsiung—are also situated there. The western coastline is lined with tidal flats and swamps.

At the southernmost point in Taiwan stands the Oluanpi Lighthouse. It was built in 1882 atop the rugged coastline to warn ships of the presence of dangerous submerged coral reefs.

RIVERS AND DRAINAGE

All of Taiwan's rivers rise in the mountains of the Central Range. The longest rivers are the Choshui at 116 miles (187 km) and the Kaoping at 106 miles (171 km). Although most of the rivers are not long, they drain a relatively large area. The Tan-shui, which flows northward toward Taipei, drains 1,052 square miles (2,725 square km); the Choshui drains 1,218 square miles (3,155 square km) of the western coastal plain; and

The Penghu islands' natural harbors once served as safe havens for pirates who attacked the Chinese coast. Today, the islands are among the world's major sources of coral.

the Kaoping drains 1,257 square miles (3,256 square km) of the southern plain near Kao-hsiung. The Wu River is only 73 miles (119 km) long and yet drains 782 square miles (2,026 square km). Many of Taiwan's rivers have been dammed to generate hydroelectricity.

ISLANDS OF TAIWAN

Known as the Pescadores (meaning Fishermen's Islands) by 16th-century Portuguese sailors, the Penghu archipelago is made up of 64 islands in the Taiwan Strait. Situated approximately midway between Taiwan and mainland China, it has a land area of 49 square miles (127 square km). Only 20 islands in the archipelago are inhabited, and almost half the total population of the main island of Penghu lives in the main town of Ma-kung. Penghu is the only Taiwanese county that is also an archipelago. Linking Penghu to nearby Paisha and Hsiyu islands is the Trans-ocean Bridge the longest inter island bridge in the Far East. Built originally in 1970, the bridge was damaged by the weather and ocean tides, and was subsequently rebuilt and reopened to the public in 1996. It now spans the length of 8,182 feet (2,494 m).

The Kinmen (Quemoy) and Matsu islands are the Taiwanese islands closest to mainland China. Kinmen is 150 miles (240 km) from Taiwan Island and only 1.4 miles (2.3 km) from mainland China, while Matsu is about 1 mile (1.6 kilometers) from the mainland. The Kinmen islands, 12 islets lying off mainland China's Fujian Province, cover a total area of 58 square miles (150 square km).

The main island in this group is the rocky and hilly Kinmen Island. The Matsu islands lie 131 miles (211 km) from northern Taiwan, off the northeast coast of Fujian Province. This island group has 19 islets, the largest of which is Nankan. Being so close to mainland China, Kinmen and Matsu are mainly military outposts, although there does exist a small nonmilitary population inhabiting both islands that fishes and farms for a living. Kinmen is also the site of a national park.

Lan-yü, or Orchid Island, is named after the profusion of wild orchids that grow on the island's hilly slopes. It has an area of 17 square miles (44 square km). Lan-yü is the home of the Yami aboriginal people, who make a living chiefly from fishing in the surrounding sea.

Taiwan's other islands include Chimei, also called the Island of Seven Beauties, south of Penghu; Hsiao Liuchiu, off southeastern Taiwan; and Lü-tao, or Green Island, off the eastern coast.

Besides these islands, Taiwan has also laid claim to two other groups of islands in the South China Sea—the Pratas and Spratly islands (called Tungsha and Nansha by the Taiwanese). The Spratly Islands are also claimed by five other Asian countries: China, Vietnam, the Philippines, Malaysia, and Brunei.

The scenic Lan-yü, or Orchid Island, once had another unofficial and sinister name—Death Island—because it was inhabited by a mite with a fatal bite.

CITIES

Close to 90 percent of the people in Taiwan live in urban centers.

TAIPEI Meaning "north Taiwan" in Mandarin, Taipei is the political, cultural, and economic center of Taiwan and its largest city. Taipei grew out of a settlement that was established in the latter half of the 1600s on the banks of the Tan-shui River. Although it gradually developed in

Taipei's park is a green haven in a congested and overpopulated city.

the centuries that followed, Taipei remained a provincial and relatively underdeveloped town; even as late as the 1950s, many rice and vegetable farms could be found within the city limits. Few now remain.

The economic prosperity of the 1970s and 1980s saw the construction of many modern high-rise buildings. The current tallest building in the world, Taipei 101, is located in this city. Present-day Taipei is a cosmopolitan city of 2.6 million people.

KAO-HSIUNG In the southwest, facing the South China Sea, Kao-hsiung is Taiwan's second largest city. It is an important shipping center and harbor, with a population of 1.5 million. Besides being Taiwan's biggest international seaport, Kao-hsiung and its environs are also Taiwan's most important industrial areas, with heavy industries dealing in petrochemicals, cement, shipbuilding, steel, oil, and sugar refining. Recent trends, however, have shown that Taiwan's economy is becoming increasingly dependent on high-tech industries located mostly in the north, especially in the three counties near Taipei City: T'ao-yüan County, T'ai-pei County, and Hsin-chu County.

T'AI-CHUNG T'ai-chung, which means central Taiwan, is the country's third largest city, with close to 1 million people. It is located midway along the North-South Highway that runs from Taipei to Kao-hsiung and is an important industrial city, producing a wide range of manufactured goods. T'ai-chung was founded in 1721 and was first called Tatun by settlers from mainland China. Since 1976 it has become an important seaport, with the development of a harbor west of the city.

T'ai-chung was given its present name in 1895 during the Japanese occupation of Taiwan.

T'AI-NAN T'ai-nan, the oldest city in Taiwan, served as the country's capital from 1684 to 1887. It is the fourth largest city in Taiwan today and is well known as a cultural and historic center.

CHIA-I The city of Chia-i lies on the western coastal plain. It is a small municipality that has some manufacturing industries. It functions mainly as a departure point for excursions to the Central Mountain Range, especially to Ali Shan.

CLIMATE

As Taiwan is surrounded by warm ocean currents, it has a warm climate. The northern region tends to be cooler than the south, so it is often said that Taiwan's climate is subtropical in the north and tropical in the south. During the hot, humid summers that last from May to September, the temperature reaches 80–95°F (27–34°C). December through February is wintertime, with mild temperatures of 54–61°F (12–16°C). Because the winters are very mild, snow hardly ever falls in Taiwan except in parts of the Central Mountain Range.

Taiwan's weather pattern is greatly affected by the monsoons. The northeast monsoon brings heavy winds and rain from the East China Sea from October through March. Usually the northeast region and the eastern coast are the most heavily affected, although people living on the west

Raincoats and umbrellas offer little protection to the residents of Taipei as strong wind and rain from Typhoon Haitang (2005) batters the city.

SUN MOON LAKE

One of the most famous lakes in Taiwan is Sun Moon Lake. According to legend, it was once two separate lakes—Sun Lake and Moon Lake—but earth tremors caused the two lakes to merge together. Ever since then, it has been called Sun Moon Lake. At times, some turbulence and earth movements can still be felt in the lake, causing the water to shoot up as high as 20 feet (6 m) into the air. Indeed, Taiwan's geography continues to be reshaped in a similar fashion today. An earthquake on September 21, 1999, created a new lake in the central mountains and caused a slight rise in the altitudes of some mountain summits.

coast also have to take precautions. During the southwest monsoon from May to September, the situation is reversed so that southern Taiwan has wet weather and northern Taiwan is drier. Rainfall in Taiwan is high, at about 100 inches (254 cm) per year.

"Taipei's weather is like a stepmother's temper" is a common complaint by many of Taipei's residents, who have to put up with high humidity and constant rain. Because Taipei is ringed by mountains that trap moisture, summers are uncomfortably hot and humid; in winter, a light drizzle can persist for weeks on end.

TYPHOONS—TERROR FROM THE SEAS

Every July to September, Taiwan does battle with typhoons and tropical cyclones called *tai fong* (TAI fohng). The most recent typhoon to hit Taiwan made landfall on Taiwan on October 2, 2005. These typhoons are usually summertime phenomena, when strong, violent winds of up to 100 miles (161 km) per hour and driving rain sweep across the country. An average of three typhoons hit Taiwan every year, and the southern and eastern regions are usually the most badly affected.

In 1968 Taiwan was hit by one of the worst typhoons in living memory. Torrential rains caused floods and landslides that killed many people and damaged millions of dollars' worth of property and crops. People thought at the time that no other typhoon could be as bad—then another terror from the seas struck in August 1994. In this typhoon the flooding was so severe that in some areas floodwaters were over 10 feet (3 m) high and reached the second stories of some buildings. Typhoon Toraji in 2001 also had a considerable impact on Taiwan, causing over 200 casualties and serious damage from flooding and landslides.

Typhoons have become so much a part of life in Taiwan that people automatically prepare for them. Taiwan's International Community Radio Taipei and Weather Control Bureau constantly monitor and advise the public on the status of typhoons by publishing condition alerts:

Condition 24:   Typhoons may hit in 24 hours.
Condition 12:   Typhoons may hit in 12 hours.
Condition 8:   Typhoons may hit in 8 hours.
Emergency Alert: Typhoons have hit the island.

During typhoon alerts the island comes to a standstill as people stay at home to ride out the storm. In homes, people prepare for floods and winds by packing up or securing loose items. Because electrical power can fail if power lines are knocked down, people stock up on batteries and candles. Extra drinking water and food are also stored in case of emergencies—even after a typhoon has blown itself out, there is still a real risk of landslides and floods.

TAIWAN'S NATIONAL FLOWER

The *Prunus mei*, or plum blossom, is the national flower of Taiwan. It has a delicate fragrance and comes in pastel shades of pink and white. The *mei* blossom is a hardy flower. Because it blooms in winter, it has come to symbolize perseverance and courage for the Taiwanese.

FLORA AND FAUNA

Taiwan's flora, which is similar to that of mainland China, varies with the altitude. In lowland regions below 2,000 feet (610 m), palm and other evergreen trees are found. The most common tree is the acacia. Mangroves are abundant in tidal areas, and bamboo flourishes all over the island, especially in the areas that receive the highest rainfall. Cedars, maples, and cypresses can be found up to 7,000 feet (2,130 m), and coniferous alpine forests do well at the highest elevations. Forests cover 55 percent of the island, mostly in the mountains of the Central Range.

Urbanization and industrialization have taken their toll on the wildlife of Taiwan. Habitat destruction due to land development, pollution, excessive hunting, and logging has led to a dramatic reduction in the population of wild animals. Wildlife conservation was neglected during Taiwan's years of industrial development in the 1960s and 1970s.

In the 1980s mounting public awareness led to greater government action in protecting and conserving wildlife. In 1981 nine nature reserves were created to protect flora and fauna, and in 1983 the export of all native wildlife was banned.

Taiwan now has a multitiered conservation system involving six national parks (Taroko, Yü Shan, K'en-ting, Yang-ming-shan, Shei-Pa, and Kinmen), 19 nature reserves, nine forest reserves, and 16 wildlife refuges. Lan-yü was slated to be Taiwan's seventh national park, but this did not happen because of opposition from the island's aborigines.

The Taroko National Park is one of the areas set aside for the conservation of indigenous flora.

This Taiwan tree frog was spotted in a wildlife sanctuary.

Taiwan's Wildlife Conservation Act was passed in 1989 to protect endangered species as well as rare and valuable wildlife. It has become increasingly difficult to sight predatory animals such as the Formosan black bear, the largest mammal in Taiwan, and the palm civet. The clouded leopard has been classified as an endangered species. Other animals that have suffered a reduction in population are the spotted deer and Swinhoe's deer. Among the animals more commonly found are wild boar, foxes, monkeys, and goats.

Taiwan also has a very abundant native and migratory bird life due to its strategic location. The country lies at the crossroads of a major migration route for birds escaping the cold winters of northeast Asia, and also for birds from Japan and the eastern coastal areas of China and Siberia migrating southward to the warmer climate of Southeast Asia. Thus, besides its own considerable number of resident bird species, Taiwan is also a major stopover and important pit stop for hundreds of other migratory birds. It is this rich diversity of wildlife that Taiwan's growing conservation movement aims to preserve.

WHICH HAS PRIORITY?

In 1991 a survey was conducted involving some 2,400 Taiwanese. They were asked the question: "Which should be given priority—environmental protection or economic growth?" Of those who responded, 11 percent chose economic growth, 37 percent chose environmental protection, 43 percent believed both were possible, and 9 percent were not sure.

CLEANING UP TAIWAN: WITH PUBLIC POLICIES OR CIVIL EDUCATION?

Where the environmental health of Taiwan is concerned, there has been some effort to cultivate a conservation ethic among the general populace, with the aim of preventing further environmental deterioration and regaining economic vitality.

Rapid economic growth achieved through industrialization has come at a price for Taiwan, threatening the very survival of the country's indigenous wildlife. Air, water, and noise pollutions are slowly but surely killing off native vegetation and animals in Taiwan. The ultimate cost of these pollutions to the country's flora and fauna has increasingly impinged on the government's and public's consciousness. Consequently, there is a growing environmental consciousness and proactive movement in the country to protect its ecological systems.

On its part the government promotes the use of environmentally friendly products and pushes for the elimination of convenient but nonrecyclable products from the citizens' daily life. The strict enforcement of environment conservation and protection laws coupled with a sustained campaign to educate the public on the consequences of pollution has inculcated an environmentally protective ethic among the public. At the forefront of the conservation movement is the Council of Agriculture, which has sponsored research projects, organized international symposia, and subsidized publicity campaigns, while having commissioned other government agencies to provide conservation-related publications.

HISTORY

ALTHOUGH TRACES OF HUMAN REMAINS and settlements have been found in Taiwan dating back 10,000 years, very little is known about these early settlers. It has been suggested that these are the remains of people from southern China, which, at that time, might have been linked to Taiwan by a land bridge. These primitive people, who left evidence of a Stone Age culture, died out mysteriously around 5,000 years ago. Later waves of migrants and settlers, in particular the aboriginal people and the Han Chinese, left more lasting impacts on Taiwan.

THE ABORIGINAL SETTLERS

Early records from mainland China from the third century A.D. noted the presence of aboriginal peoples living along the coast of Taiwan. Of Austronesian stock, the aborigines are believed to have migrated to Taiwan from Southeast Asia.

The early aboriginal people belonged to a number of groups and were mainly fishermen, hunters, and farmers. Apart from occasional intertribal warfare, they lived peacefully until their existence was disrupted by the arrival of the mainland Chinese in the 13th century A.D.

EARLY CONTACTS WITH CHINA

Although Taiwan's history is often tied to that of mainland China, the early Chinese emperors considered Taiwan to be outside their sphere of influence. The earliest record of mainland China's contact with Taiwan dates back to A.D. 239, when an expeditionary naval force was sent to explore Taiwan. From the seventh century onward, Chinese naval forces sent patrols to Taiwan to police the seas separating the island from the

Above: **Typical boat decoration of the Yami, an aboriginal people who inhabited Taiwan for over 1,000 years before the first Chinese people arrived on the island.**

Opposite: **A pottery artifact belonging to the early immigrants who settled in Taiwan.**

23

DYNASTIES OF CHINA

Throughout its 4,000 years of history, mainland China has had a succession of ruling families, called dynasties. Taiwan's history has been closely associated with China since the time it was declared a Chinese protectorate during the Yuan dynasty.

Xia dynasty	21st–16th century B.C.	Sui dynasty	581–618
Shang dynasty	16th century–1066 B.C.	Tang dynasty	618–907
Zhou dynasty	1066–221 B.C.	The Five dynasties	907–960
Qin dynasty	221–206 B.C.	Sung dynasty	A.D. 960–1127
Han dynasty	206 B.C.–A.D. 23	Yuan dynasty	1271–1368
The Three Kingdoms	A.D. 220–265	Ming dynasty	1368–1644
Jin dynasty	265–420	Qing dynasty	1644–1911
Southern dynasty	420–589	Republic of China	1912–49
Northern dynasty	386–581	People's Republic of China	1949

The earliest Portuguese sailors who set foot on Taiwan were so impressed with the lush beauty of the country's dramatic mountains and lovely coastal scenery that they called it Ilha Formosa, meaning Beautiful Island. Part of this name stuck, and for centuries after this, Taiwan was widely known in the West as the island of Formosa.

mainland. These were not attempts to assert control of Taiwan but actions to protect Chinese trading ships in the area from attacks by pirates.

During the Yuan dynasty (1271–1368), Taiwan was declared a protectorate of the Mongol empire by the Mongol emperor Kublai Khan (1215–94). It was around this time that the first waves of Chinese immigrants began arriving in Taiwan. Coming mostly from the Fujian and Guangdong provinces in China, they first settled along Taiwan's western coastal plains. They were followed by another wave of immigrants from Fujian Province in the 14th and 15th centuries, during the Ming dynasties (1368–1644). These and later waves of settlers caused severe disruption to the aborigines, who were either absorbed into the migrant populations, or forced to leave their villages in the plains and retreat to the mountains and the remote east coast. The migrants claimed land from the aborigines and cultivated crops such as rice and sugarcane. As these settlers prospered, Taiwan, in turn, became an important trading area.

EUROPEAN ARRIVAL

In the 16th century, drawn by the prosperous trade of the region, the Portuguese, Spanish, and Dutch began to take an interest in Taiwan.

The Portuguese, the first to arrive in the 1500s, named the island Ilha Formosa. Then, in 1624, the Dutch invaded Taiwan and set up a trading post at T'ai-nan. They also built forts to reinforce their military strength. The most famous are Fort Zeelandia and Fort Provintia. Later, the Spanish landed on the northern part of Taiwan and set up a fortified commercial post at Chi-lung and later at Tan-shui. The Dutch seized the Spanish settlements and drove them out in 1641. In this way, the Dutch extended their influence from the initial southwestern region to the northern regions as well.

The Dutch remained the colonial masters of Taiwan for less than a quarter of a century until they were themselves expelled from Taiwan in 1662 by Cheng Cheng Kung (Koxinga), a loyal general of the Ming dynasty.

KOXINGA

Meanwhile, the fall of the Ming dynasty in mainland China prompted an influx of refugees into Taiwan in 1644. One of these refugees was Cheng Cheng Kung, better known as Koxinga.

A general and warlord in the Ming dynasty, Cheng (1624–62) remained loyal to the Ming emperor in the face of the dynasty's collapse and the rise of Manchu Qing power. In recognition of his loyalty and courage, the Ming emperor granted Cheng the honor of using the royal family's surname, and Cheng then became known as Kuo Hsing-yeh, or Koxinga, Lord of the Imperial Surname.

After resisting the Manchu advance for as long as he could, Koxinga finally retreated to Taiwan along with his remaining troops and warships.

An old fort at Tan-shui built by the Spanish who occupied the town in the 17th century. Tan-shui is situated where the Tan-shui River meets the Taiwan Strait.

Koxinga was not only a warrior but also a capable political leader, an able administrator, a zealous guardian of Chinese culture, and a committed social reformer. A shrine is devoted to him in T'a-inan.

He planned to drive the Dutch out of Taiwan and set up a base from which to overthrow the Manchus. A year later, in 1662, the Dutch surrendered control of Fort Zeelandia, their last stronghold in Taiwan (Fort Provintia had earlier been seized by Koxinga). With the end of Dutch colonial occupation, Koxinga became the ruler of Taiwan.

Today, Koxinga is regarded as a national hero and a *chun tzu* (JU-EEN tzoo), meaning perfect man, in Taiwan. His son and grandson carried on the Cheng name as rulers of Taiwan until 1683, when Manchu forces from the mainland took control of the island. Taiwan became a prefecture of Fujian Province in 1684.

JAPANESE OCCUPATION

Taiwan remained under Manchu rule for the next 212 years, although its actual hold on the territory was nominal. Except for a brief period in 1884–85, when the French occupied parts of northern Taiwan and the Penghu islands, Manchu reign was left relatively intact until 1895, when the Japanese occupied Taiwan. In 1894 the Sino-Japanese War broke out over a dispute about the status of Korea. China lost the war and in 1895 was forced to hand over control of Taiwan to Japan under the Treaty of Shimonoseki. This marked the beginning of the Japanese occupation of the island. Initially, the Taiwanese resisted the Japanese and declared their island a republic, but this insurgency was soon crushed.

Japanese rule lasted from 1895 to 1945 and brought about many changes to Taiwan as the new colonists set about improving the infrastructure of the country, building roads, railroads, schools, ports, and other facilities. This, in turn, improved Taiwan's economy. Agricultural schemes were promoted, and agricultural production boomed. As a result, Taiwan became a major exporter of rice and sugar. With the development of hydroelectric dams in 1903, industry was also given a boost. Coal mining, forestry, and iron and steel industries added to Taiwan's development during the 50 years it remained under Japan's rule.

However, there was a negative side to the Japanese occupation of Taiwan as the Japanese tried to crush nationalist feelings among the population, usually with harsh methods. Pro-China sentiments were also suppressed, and use of the Chinese language was discouraged in favor of Japanese. Japanese became the language of instruction in schools, and all official and business correspondence was required to be conducted in Japanese. During World War II many Taiwanese were forcibly conscripted into the Japanese army. The Japanese occupation came to an end with Japan's defeat in World War II, and the return of Taiwan to China in 1945.

TURMOIL IN CHINA

While Taiwan was occupied by the Japanese, a great upheaval was taking place in China. In 1911 the last Manchu Qing emperor was deposed in a revolution led by Dr. Sun Yat-sen, and China became the Republic of China (ROC). When Sun found he could not gather widespread support for himself, he stepped aside for Yuan Shih-kai to become president of the republic. Yuan declared himself emperor in 1915 but died shortly after. China plunged into further turmoil, with the former warlords of the Qing dynasty competing for control. For some years a state of civil war

Instances of harsh Japanese rule in Taiwan caused some bitterness and resentment among the Taiwanese. During the Japanese occupation, in some Taiwanese communities, when a person died, his or her casket was carried to the graveyard under a black umbrella so that the deceased person would not be buried under a Japanese sun. Nevertheless, many Taiwanese still regard the Japanese period as a progressive era in their history, particularly in comparison with later Chinese Nationalist rule.

27

Chiang Kai-shek, a political leader in the nationalist campaign against the Communists on mainland China, left China for Taiwan in 1949. He was Taiwan's president from 1949 until 1975.

prevailed, although the Nationalists (the Kuomintang party, or KMT) led by Sun managed to regain control of the southern provinces by 1923.

In 1928 General Chiang Kai-shek of the KMT defeated the northern warlords and unified China. But China continued to be destabilized by a growing Communist movement. In 1931 Japan invaded Manchuria in northern China, and by 1937 had overrun China's eastern seaboard in 1945. From a base deep in China's western heartland, the ROC fought a war of resistance, receiving aid from the Western Allied nations after the outbreak of World War II. When Japan was defeated, all of its colonies and captured territories reverted back to their previous status. This meant that Taiwan, formerly part of the Qing empire before 1895, came under the control of the Republic of China.

Even after Japan's defeat in the war, China continued to be plagued by political upheaval, this time due to a struggle for power between the Nationalists and the Communists. In 1949, the Nationalists were dealt the final blow when the Communists led by Mao Zedong captured power. General Chiang, the KMT, and a total of 1.5 million Nationalist sympathizers fled the Chinese mainland to take refuge in Taiwan.

INVASION THREATS FROM CHINA

After the KMT's retreat to Taiwan, it appeared the Communists would proceed to invade the island. However, the new Communist government was preoccupied with destroying Nationalist pockets on the mainland and postponed the invasion of Taiwan.

POLITICAL GIANTS OF CHINA AND TAIWAN

DR. SUN YAT-SEN Revered by the Taiwanese as the founding father of the Republic of China, Dr. Sun Yat-sen (pictured here with his wife) made his greatest political contribution by overthrowing the weak and corrupt Qing dynasty and introducing democratic ideals to China. Born in 1866 in China's Guangdong Province, Sun spent some years studying in Hawaii before returning to China and qualifying as a doctor in Hong Kong.

He was very much aware of the corruption inherent in the imperial system. In 1894 he formed the Hsing-chung Hui (Revive China Society), which aimed to end imperial rule and introduce democratic government, but did not meet with success. Sun then spent the next 16 years in political exile. He tried on at least 10 occasions to topple the imperial court, without success. On October 10, 1911, his followers succeeded in capturing Hubei Province in an armed uprising. Eventually, other provinces and cities joined the Nationalists and declared independence from imperial rule. Sun was elected president in December 1911 and inaugurated on January 1, 1912. During this time he reorganized his supporters to form the Kuomintang (KMT), or the Nationalist Party. Sun spent the remainder of his life fighting to unify China. He died in 1925 at the age of 59.

GENERAL CHIANG KAI-SHEK Chiang was born in 1887 to a family with a business background. Like many other young men of his time, he went to Japan to attend a military academy. And, like other young men, he became an antiimperialist. In 1905 he cut off his pigtail in defiance of the Manchus. At the time, the pigtail was regarded as a symbol of Manchu rule and oppression. In 1908 he joined Sun Yat-sen's revolutionary group. After the 1911 revolution he became a major figure in the Nationalist army.

With the death of Sun Yat-sen, Chiang became one of the party leaders of the KMT and the "generalissimo," or commander-in-chief of the National Revolutionary Army. In 1927 he married Soong Mei-ling, the sister of Sun Yat-sen's wife. A year later, he became the president of the Chinese Nationalist government. After World War II, Chiang continued his struggle against the Communists but lost the battle for the Chinese mainland. From 1949 onward, Chiang was the president of the Republic of China on Taiwan. Although he spoke often about his sacred mission of reunifying China, he was unable to fulfill his vision before he died in 1975.

A signboard in Taipei carries political cartoons showing Communist atrocities and Taiwanese patriotic deeds.

When the Korean War erupted in 1950, President Harry S. Truman of the United States ordered the U.S. Seventh Fleet to patrol the Taiwan Strait and protect Taiwan against attack from China. This act was vitally important at this dangerous time because it was the presence of such a military force that kept the Communists from invading Taiwan. Since that time, Taiwan has been treading a thin political line with China. With financial and military backing from the United States, Taiwan was able to keep China at bay in the 1950s and 1960s in spite of the Communists' continued threat to invade the island.

During these years Taiwan maintained its international status as a member of the United Nations (UN). It also claimed to be the rightful government of China, arguing that the Communists had seized the country by force, whereas the ROC was an elected government. Many nations, including the United States, accepted and supported this claim. China, on the other hand, declared that it was the legitimate government of all China, including Taiwan. Then, in the 1970s, the United States began a policy that helped it to forge a more cordial relationship with the People's Republic of China (PRC), established in 1949 after the Kuomintang fled to Taiwan. The United States established diplomatic relations with the PRC in 1979 and severed its diplomatic relations with Taiwan.

TAIWAN'S POLITICAL STATUS TODAY

For the past four decades, Taiwan and mainland China have fought a diplomatic battle on the international stage, each not recognizing the

PRESIDENT CHEN SHUI-BIAN'S CHANGING STANCE ON TAIWAN-CHINA RELATIONS

Inaugural speech on May 20, 2000

"As long as the CCP regime has no intention to use military force against Taiwan, I pledge that during my term in office, I will not declare independence. . . . I will not promote a referendum to change the status quo in regards to the question of independence or unification."

National Day Rally address on October 10, 2003

"The 'door to cooperation' and the 'door to peace' will always exist between the two sides of the Taiwan Strait. The 'door to cooperation' can open only if the 'one China' and [the] 'one country, two systems' formulas are put aside. The 'door to peace' can open only when China renounces its threat of force and halts its strategic attempts to isolate Taiwan internationally."

Inaugural Speech on May 20, 2004

"If both sides are willing, on the basis of goodwill, to create an environment engendered upon 'peaceful development and freedom of choice,' then in the future, the Republic of China and the People's Republic of China—or Taiwan and China—can seek to establish relations in any form whatsoever. We would not exclude any possibility, so long as there is the consent of the 23 million people of Taiwan."

status of the other. This division between the "two Chinas" has been a sensitive issue. Nevertheless, there has been no large-scale military conflict between the two, although there were incidents in the 1950s and 1960s when the Chinese bombed the Taiwanese islands of Matsu and Kinmen, and the Taiwanese shelled the mainland from these two islands. However, since 1968 the only instances of military antagonism between mainland China and Taiwan have come in the form of missile tests and military exercises. Nevertheless, the issue has been kept alive in propaganda campaigns in both mainland China and Taiwan.

With each side claiming to be "the real China," Taiwan's political status has often taken a beating. In 1971 the UN recognized the PRC as the government of China, costing Taiwan its seat in the UN. Since then, and especially as the United States and other nations are on increasingly cordial terms with mainland China, Taiwan has had to work hard to uphold its status in the international arena. In 1991 Taiwan's president,

In 1991 the government of the Republic of China on Taiwan renounced the use of force to achieve national unification with the mainland. However, China has not yet renounced the use of force against Taiwan in spite of the growing economic ties between both countries in recent years.

Lee Teng-hui, declared that the Republic of China on Taiwan would no longer claim to be the government of mainland China. He conceded that the People's Republic of China exercised the powers of government in the mainland areas and announced that the Taiwanese government would no longer try to use force to restore its power over the mainland.

There are some Taiwanese who take a more radical position: they think Taiwan should give up on the idea of unifying with the mainland. Instead, they believe that Taiwan should become completely independent from China. Many advocates of Taiwanese independence believe a declaration of independence is necessary or think that changing the country's name from "Republic of China" to "Republic of Taiwan" is a better idea.

The idea of an independent Taiwan is unacceptable to the People's Republic of China, which has promised to use force, if necessary, to prevent Taiwan from cutting its ties to China. Even though the two sides are not governed by the same authorities today, supporters of unification believe they should be in the future. A declaration of independence would make the establishment of a single ruling government much more difficult. The PRC government would like Taiwan to become part of China, with the central government in Beijing, but China's leaders say Taiwan could keep its own political and economic system. This formula is called "one country, two systems."

By and large, however, most Taiwanese citizens are not very eager for either unification or independence. Frequent public opinion surveys taken over the past 20 years show that support for unification, at least in the near future, is declining. Nevertheless, support for independence is also weak. Most Taiwanese prefer to keep things the way they are: keeping their own, separate political and economic systems, but not ruling out the possibility of unification in the future.

Taiwan's leaders have a difficult job balancing the desire of Taiwanese citizens for a government of their own with the PRC's insistence that Taiwan move toward unification. Since the early 1990s growing economic ties between the two sides have made some things easier and others more complicated. Many Taiwanese and Chinese work together and enjoy shared prosperity. On the other hand, because of the differing political stances of the two governments, even simple tasks are difficult. For example, as late as 2006 it was not possible to fly a plane directly from Taiwan to China and back. Travelers had to take a long detour, usually through Hong Kong, to make the short trip.

TAIWAN-CHINA RELATIONS

In the early years of the 21st century, both sides of the Taiwan Strait have been influenced by events taking place domestically and internationally. The unprecedented change of the governing party in Taiwan in 2000 brought its democratization movement to new heights. Extraneous changes and transitions are taking place in China's economic and political spheres. Cross-strait interactions, which began with family visits in 1987, have increased rapidly, especially since the concurrent accession of both countries to the World Trade Organization (WTO). On the global front, the election of a new U.S. administration in 2000 has led to adjustments to America's foreign policy toward Asia. The September 11, 2001, terrorist attacks in the United States have also changed the way countries around the world engage one another. All these developments have enlarged the impact of Taiwan-China relations—taking them from regional waters out to the high seas of international relations. The onus is now on both countries to seek new perspectives on an age-old issue and to coexist and prosper in the international arena.

In 2003 Taiwan approved of indirect chartered flights to and from China to meet the increased volume of Taiwanese traveling home from the mainland during the 15-day Lunar New Year festival. Only Taiwan's airlines and foreign carriers were allowed to take part. A total of 3,556 seats were provided, and while 1,322 Taiwanese registered for the flight, 2,462 people were actually carried home.

—Taiwan-China relations, Taiwan Yearbook 2004

GOVERNMENT

IN ITS EARLY YEARS in Taiwan, the Kuomintang (KMT) took steps to strengthen its position as the Nationalist government of China. Martial law was imposed, and elections for the legislature, presidency, and other political offices were suspended. Although it was argued that this contravened the democratic principles of the constitution, the KMT justified its policy on the grounds that it was necessary in the face of emergency conditions and the threat of invasion from the mainland.

In the 1970s some Taiwanese citizens began agitating for the relaxation of these restrictions and for permission for more democratic practices. Democracy activists wrote books and magazines to publicize their ideas, took part in local elections and even won a few seats in the ROC legislature. In what is now known as the Kao-hsiung Incident of 1979, a group of activists clashed with the police during a demonstration, leading to the arrest and imprisonment of a number of democracy activists.

Forty years of martial law ended in 1987 when the KMT began to liberalize under the leadership of President Chiang Ching-kuo. Political parties were formed, and the democratic process envisioned by Dr. Sun Yat-sen came into being. In May 1991 President Lee Teng-hui announced

"The Republic of China, founded on the Three Principles of the People, shall be a democratic republic of the people, to be governed by the people, and for the people."

—*Article 1 of the Constitution of the Republic of China, 1947*

Opposite: **A soldier salutes in front of a statue of Chiang Kai-shek.**

THE THREE PRINCIPLES OF THE PEOPLE

The Three Principles of the People form the basis of the 1947 Constitution of the Republic of China on Taiwan. They were formulated by Dr. Sun Yat-sen, who was influenced by democratic philosophies in Western countries, especially the United States, where he lived for some time. The principles are: nationalism—independence for China, equality for all ethnic groups, and a sense of national identity in a common culture; democracy—political and civil liberties for each individual, and governing power to the organs of government; and social well-being—building a prosperous and just society where wealth is equitably distributed.

the end of the Period of National Mobilization for Suppression of the Communist Rebellion. The first general elections to the legislative *yuan* (YOO-ahn), meaning council, and the National Assembly were held in December of that same year.

Taiwan's government is sectioned into central, municipal, and country-city levels. The *yuan* together with the office of the president make up the central government. The National Assembly, on the other hand, was a body whose functions were to ratify constitutional amendments and territorial changes to the public through referendums. It was abolished in 2005. Taiwan today has a national government with a president, five *yuan*, and 25 country and city governments. The most important government officials are the president, the premier (who heads the cabinet) and the legislators (the lawmakers).

FIVE BRANCHES OF NATIONAL GOVERNMENT

Most democratic countries have three branches of national government; Taiwan is unique in having five: executive, legislative, judicial, examination, and control. The executive *yuan* functions as the national policy-making body, equivalent to a cabinet. It has a number of ministries, commissions, and councils, and is headed by a premier. The premier is appointed by the president and sanctioned by the legislative *yuan*. The legislative *yuan* is a single-chamber parliament and the highest lawmaking body. In 2005 the legislative *yuan* had 225 seats, but this will be reduced to 113 seats in 2007. In the past decade it has become more powerful—evolving from merely passing laws sponsored by the KMT into an active forum for debate and policy development. It also has responsibility for initiating constitutional amendments.

The judicial *yuan* is responsible for the legal system, which is composed of the Supreme Court, high courts, district courts, and administrative courts. It also has the power of judicial review, under which it interprets the constitution and ensures that government action is carried out according to the constitution.

Besides these three conventional branches of government, Taiwan has two more unusual ones. The examination *yuan* is responsible for the examination, employment, and management of the civil service. The control *yuan* is a watchdog that audits or checks on the activities of the other branches of government and has the power to censure and impeach government officials.

NATIONAL ASSEMBLY

The president is the head of state and is directly elected by the people every four years. During the years of martial law, when a state of emergency existed in Taiwan, the president was elected by a body called the National Assembly. After President Chiang Kai-shek's death in 1975, he was succeeded by his vice president, Yen Chia Kan. In 1978 Chiang

Martial law is often declared when a country is deemed to be in a state of emergency, often due to war, a major natural disaster, a coup d'état, or civil disorder. In such instances military organizations are given control over the normal adminstrations of justice. Instituting martial law often involves restricting citizens' rights and imposing curfews.

Ching-kuo, son of Chiang Kai-shek, became president. In 1988 he was succeeded by Lee Teng-hui, the first native Taiwanese to become president. In 1996 Taiwan held its first popular presidential election. Lee Teng-hui was elected again, this time by the people of Taiwan. Lee Teng-hui was then succeeded by Chen Shui-bian of the Democratic Progressive Party (DPP) in 2000. The next presidential elections are due to be held in 2008.

Until it was abolished in 2005, the National Assembly's powers were limited to electing the president and vice president and amending the constitution. The first elections to the National Assembly took place in 1947 when 2,961 delegates were elected to serve a six-year term. However, after martial law was imposed in 1949, elections to the Assembly were suspended, and the original delegates now found themselves "frozen" in office. When Taiwan adopted direct presidential elections in 1994, the National Assembly's primary function was lost, and so led to its abolishment.

POLITICAL PARTIES

From 1949 to 1987, when all political parties other than the KMT were banned, Taiwan's government was effectively a one-party system. The first sign of political liberalization came in 1986 when the DPP was formed. Since then, the political system has been increasingly democratized and liberalized into a competitive party system. With the ban on opposition parties lifted, over 60 political parties sprouted up in Taiwan. By April 1993 Taiwan had 73 political parties and 23 political organizations.

Up to 2000 the KMT had controlled the government for 51 years until the DPP took over. In 2001 the DPP became the largest party in the legislative *yuan* followed by the KMT. Other prominent political parties in Taiwan include the Taiwan Solidarity Union and the People First Party.

COUNTY AND CITY GOVERNMENTS

Taiwan is divided into 18 counties called *hsien* (SEE-en). Each *hsien* has urban townships called *chen* (jehn) and rural townships called *hsiang* (SEE-ahng). Each county and municipality also has an elected executive (mayor) and council. Taipei and Kao-hsiung are considered special municipalities, and each has a mayor. The mayors of these special municipalities are elected by popular vote.

Kao-hsiung is a special municipality. This status can only be conferred if the county or municipality has over 1.25 million people and if specific political, economic, and cultural developments have taken place.

When the DPP was founded, it was technically illegal, but the decision to lift the ban against political parties less than a year later made the party lawful.

ECONOMY

OVER THE PAST 40 YEARS Taiwan has achieved a degree of economic success that has made it the envy of countries around the world. From being a relatively poor economy dependent on agriculture as its main source of income, Taiwan is now an Asian Dragon—a newly industrializing economy that has made the leap from manufacturing low-technology goods such as toys and clothes to manufacturing high-technology computers and aerospace systems.

Much of Taiwan's spectacular economic growth has been due to an export-oriented strategy and the development of its infrastructure. This started in the 1960s with the manufacture and export of low-cost, mass-produced consumer products. In the 1970s the economy shifted into high gear with the development of heavy industries. Ten major infrastructure projects, including the construction of highways, railways, harbors, and an international airport, were undertaken, boosting the economy.

In the 1980s Taiwan faced rising land and labor costs that affected its competitive position in Asia. As the New Taiwan (NT) dollar appreciated in value, many Taiwanese companies, especially in labor-intensive industries, began to shift their operations to countries with lower costs. To counter this, Taiwan made fresh ventures in its overseas investment. In 2002 China, including its Special Administrative Region (SAR) of Hong Kong, was the recipient of two-thirds of Taiwanese investment. The top five industries for Taiwanese investment are banking and finance, electronic and electrical appliances, services, international trade, and transportation.

NATIONAL DEVELOPMENT PLAN

Economic development in the 1990s was driven by the Six-Year National Development Plan launched by the government in 1991. A large-scale investment of over $300 billion in more than 600 projects was planned for a

Opposite: **This compound is one of the many industrial sites that have sprung up in Taiwan over the last few decades as a result of the rapid industrialization taking place on the island.**

A worker at China Ship-building Corporation in Kao-hsiung, a major seaport and industrial capital in Taiwan.

number of sectors, including mass transit, the transportation industry, telecommunications, power generation, and environmental protection. Besides raising national income and upgrading the quality of life, the development plan aimed to raise Taiwan's status to that of a developed economy—a goal that was realized in 2002 when the country was admitted into the WTO as a developed country.

CONSTRUCTION

In the 1970s and 1980s the construction sector focused on public infrastructure projects that provided a boost to economic growth as well as laying the foundation for industrial development. The Six-Year National Development Plan aimed to rectify Taiwan's housing shortage with the construction of 900,000 housing units. To balance out such a high concentration of construction projects in the cities, the government created 18 regional development areas, each having an industrial base, public facilities, and a transportation network.

Infrastructure and development were also an important component of Taiwan's development plan. Taipei's subway system was one such project. It consists of four lines: the Western Railway, the Hua-lien-T'ai-tung Line, the Yilan Line, and the North Link Line, and has been up and running for several years. Construction of the Kao-hsiung mass rapid transit (MRT) system is underway with partial operation expected in April 2007. A second north-south highway and other east-west highways are planned, while a high-speed railway link between Taipei in the north and Kao-hsiung in the south was recently completed. Three of Taiwan's international ports have established free trade port zones since 2004: Chi-lung Port, Kao-hsiung Port, and T'ai-chung Port. In 2005 plans were drawn up to link the Chiang Kai-shek International Airport in T'ao-yüan with Taipei City. More nuclear power plants are also planned to boost the production of energy.

SEAPORTS

Taiwan's four international seaports are located in Chi-lung, Kao-hsiung, Hua-lien, and T'ai-chung. In 2003 Kao-hsiung was one of the top 10 busiest ports (measured in terms of container traffic), with Chi-lung trailing behind in 33rd position. T'ai-chung handles goods traded from central Taiwan and is expected to develop into the main trading harbor for exports and imports with the People's Republic of China (PRC), while Hua-lien handles much of Taiwan's cross-Pacific trade.

TRADE

Trade is Taiwan's lifeblood. Due to the political dispute between mainland China and Taiwan, direct trade between the two was banned until 1987. Taiwanese businesses got around this by indirectly trading with the mainland through Hong Kong. In 2005 the country was the 14th largest trading economy in the world. In 2004 its total trade amounted to $330 billion, with exports of $173 billion and imports of $157 billion. Currently, Taiwan's major trading partners are Japan, mainland China, and the United States. Taiwan has a trade surplus with the United States (more exports

A container ship docks at Chi-lung harbor, one of Taiwan's busiest ports.

than imports), and a trade deficit with Japan (more imports than exports). Trade with Southeast Asia has also increased in the past few years.

INDUSTRY

The driving force behind Taiwan's economic miracle has been its dynamic industrial sector. The manufacturing segment, in particular, is the most important part of industry and accounted for over a quarter of the country's GDP in 2004.

Among the heavy industrial goods manufactured are transportation equipment, electrical and electronic machinery, and metal and petrochemical products. Light industrial goods include beverages, tobacco, textiles, and clothing. While as much as 95 percent of Taiwan's industrial production used to be made domestically, rising wages in recent years have forced local companies to relocate—mostly to mainland China—a trend that looks to continue as barriers to trade between both countries are increasingly being eradicated. As of 2005 the service industry accounts for about two-thirds of Taiwan's GDP.

MADE IN TAIWAN

During the 1970s Taiwan's economy grew at an average annual rate of 9–10 percent, a figure most Western economies rarely achieve even in the best of times. Today it has established a name for itself as a world leader in the manufacturing of several products, ranging from consumer electronics and designer fashions to sophisticated aerospace systems.

Over the past 10 years, the biggest export markets for Taiwanese goods have shifted from the United States and Japan to China and Hong Kong. In shipbuilding, petrochemicals, and electrical and electronic products, Taiwan is home to Asia's leading industries.

However, it is in the information technology industry that Taiwan has really carved out a niche for itself. In 2004 Taiwan became the world's third largest manufacturer of hardware products for personal computers. It is also the world's fourth largest supplier of semiconductor components, catering to the global IT industry. One of Taiwan's leading computer manufacturers is Acer, which has established an international name and opened over 50 offices worldwide.

A significant portion of the money from foreign investments has gone into upgrading Taiwan's manufacturing industries, including those that produce electronic and electrical appliances and machinery.

The establishment of export processing zones in Taiwan has been an important factor in the island's industrial development. In 1966 the Kao-hsiung Export Processing Zone became the first free trade area and industrial park in Taiwan. Its success with foreign investors had important spin-offs for the economy in providing jobs and foreign exchange. Since then, two other export-processing zones have been set up near T'ai-nan and T'ai-chung counties. As of 2005 Taiwan has 57 industrial zones, among which seven zones are being developed and an additional 107,728 acres (43,596 ha) of land has been earmarked for industrial development.

As Taiwan's economy grows, the country's six-year National Development Plan for 2002–08 proposes initiatives that target several skill-intensive fields for development—some of which are the semiconductor and the "3C" industries (consumer electronics, communications, and computers). The Taiwanese government wants to see a shift in manufacturing—from developing production efficiency to emphasizing product innovation through research and development, and it has put in place the policies to encourage this.

AGRICULTURE

Although it remains a significant sector of the Taiwanese economy, agriculture has decreased considerably in importance. Contributing to

Farmers harvesting sugarcane in the fields. Taiwan's major crops include rice, sugarcane, fruits, tea, vegetables, corn, tobacco, and peanuts. There is also a livestock sector that produces pigs, poultry, dairy cattle, and fishery supplies.

one-third of the economy in 1952, it only accounted for 1.7 percent of Taiwan's GDP in 2004. In 2005 animal and vegetable product exports together contributed only about 1 percent of the country's GDP.

Low income is a major reason for the declining agricultural sector. In 2002 the average annual income of each farming household was $24,914. Only 20.5 percent of that came from agricultural activities, as nearly 80 percent of Taiwan's farming households supplemented their income with part-time jobs or had members who held full-time nonfarming jobs. As a result, an increasing number of young people are leaving the farms to work in the cities or in industry. In 2004 only 6.7 percent of the labor force was employed in the agricultural sector, about half of 1992's 12.6 percent. The shortage of farm workers and rising costs have led to an efficiency drive, and the government is promoting greater mechanization and the consolidation of small farms.

MINERAL RESOURCES

Taiwan's coal reserves of about 110 million tons are located mainly in the northern counties, and its oil and natural gas reserves are located mostly in Hsin-chu and Miao-li counties. As these mineral resources are insufficient to generate enough energy for total domestic demand, many rivers have been dammed to produce hydroelectric power. Marble, limestone, and asbestos are Taiwan's other mineral resources.

The agricultural sector faces many challenges: farm land is decreasing due to urban and industrial expansion; farming attracts few people because farmers have a lower average income compared with the nonfarming population; and tariffs on imported agricultural products are continually being lowered, causing a loss in earnings for farmers.

47

ENVIRONMENT

THE ENVIRONMENTAL CONSERVATION MOVEMENT in Taiwan is geared towards realizing the goal of "azure skies, green earth, blue mountains, and clear waters" (as articulated by the country's Environment Protection Administration—EPA). While undoing the damage caused by irresponsible economic and industrial development might not necessarily be possible, Taiwan has taken steps to prevent further damage from being inflicted on its abundant biodiversity through environmental protection and conservation efforts.

CONSERVATION LAWS, POLICIES, AND ORGANIZATIONS

The EPA is the only government agency at the national level that is solely devoted to the environmental conservation movement in Taiwan. The responsibilities of the EPA include setting standards to regulate the amount of pollution and the drafting of environmental conservation laws. As an example to the rest of the country, the EPA issued a mandate in 2002 requiring all central government agencies (including state-owned enterprises and schools) and municipal agencies to initiate "green procurement" efforts—that is, 50 percent of the supplies procured by these agencies have to be environmentally friendly. In 2002, with the implementation of such "green" purchasing measures, applications for the use of the Green Mark imprint increased nearly fourfold.

FIGHTING POLLUTION

AIR POLLUTION Taiwan's Air Pollution Control Act (enacted in 1975, revised in 2002) empowers the government to establish air-quality standards for different areas across Taiwan. The combat against air pollution heightened

Taiwan is home to approximately 150,000 different forms of life—1.5 percent of all life species found on earth—out of which 30 percent are endemic to the country. This vast variety in flora and fauna can be partially attributed to the country's location between three climatic zones and its varied topography.

Opposite: **A garbage collector walks in front of a mountain of plastic bottles that are to be sorted out for recycling.**

49

THE GREEN MARK PROGRAM

Launched by Taiwan's EPA in 1992, the Green Mark Program promotes recycling, pollution reduction, and conservation of resources. Consumer products and services bearing the Green Mark imprint signify that they are low-polluting, conserve resources, and are recyclable.

Seven years later the government singled out Green Mark products as targets for priority purchasing by consumers by allowing a maximum of 10 percent reduction on prices. In addition, the criteria for being awarded a Green Mark have been expanded to include characteristics such as energy-saving and being manufactured with regenerated materials.

with the issuance of air-quality improvement measures, which include the articulation of tough emission standards for industrial plants and motor vehicles, regular exhaust inspections for motorcycles, the promotion of low-pollution transportation vehicles, as well as imposing strict standards on the composition of petroleum products, among other measures.

The most significant effort to improve air quality in Taiwan is the introduction of the Air Pollution Control (APC) fee by the EPA in 1995. The APC fee is imposed on stationary sources of air pollution such as factories and construction sites, as well as mobile sources such as motor vehicles. The fee is based on the amount of pollutants—that is, suspended particles, nitrogen oxides, sulphur oxides, and hydrocarbons—emitted by these sources. In the fiscal year of 2002, the APC fee system generated $68 million. The fees collected are used mainly to set up and implement air pollution control programs.

Another front in Taiwan's battle against air pollution is global warming. The current emission level of greenhouse gases in Taiwan is similar to those of Organization for Economic Cooperation and Development (OECD) countries—the main producers of greenhouse gases in the world. According to the Taiwan EPA, the greenhouse gases frequently emitted by the country include carbon dioxide, methane, nitrous oxide, hydrofluorocarbons, perfluorocarbons, and sulphur hexafluoride. Carbon dioxide makes up most of these greenhouse gases.

WATER POLLUTION Taiwan has 118 rivers and streams under government supervision, 24 of which provide the country with 85 percent of the water used by its citizens. Measures to ensure water quality include setting up

The sun sets under smoke billowing from an oil refinery in Taiwan's southern city of Kao-hsiung. The Taiwanese government aims to have such industrial emissions drastically reduced in the near future.

water quality sampling stations throughout the country as well as placing 13 of these rivers on a priority watch list for five years (since 2002).

The main pollutants of Taiwan's rivers are domestic sewage and industrial discharges. Urban communities are the main polluters, primarily because of the lack of comprehensive sewage systems. In general, Taiwan has constructed less than 10 percent of its sewage system with the exception of Taipei, which has a higher degree of completion, with 77 percent of buildings in Taipei City connected to a sewage disposal or waste treatment system. Water pollution in Taiwan has left the country with poor quality drinking water. The EPA together with other government agencies has come up with a Source Water Quality Protection Plan, which is an eight-year project to protect sources of drinking water for more than 12 million people in Taiwan. To achieve this goal, 11 reservoirs were constructed at five major watersheds.

NOISE POLLUTION The increase in commercial and industrial activity that accompanied Taiwan's economic development has led to a disproportionate surge in noise complaints among the Taiwanese people. As of 2003 the EPA has received more than 20,000 cases of noise complaints per annum. Noise is currently the leading environmental problem handled by the EPA.

To protect its diverse ecosystems, the Taiwan government has set aside 19.5 percent of the country's land area as part of a multitiered conservation system composed of six national parks, 19 nature reserves, nine forest reserves, 16 wildlife refuges and 30 major wildlife habitats.

WASTE DISPOSAL AND RECYCLING

The 21 incinerators in Taiwan have the capability of processing 70 percent of the garbage produced daily in Taiwan. Fifteen more incinerators were originally planned to be built, although this has since been reduced to eight given the country's success at implementing its garbage reduction and recycling programs.

According to the EPA, about 40 percent of Taiwan's garbage is recyclable, thus spurring resource recycling and waste-reduction programs. For example, as part of the Four-in-One Resource Recycling Program, citizens are encouraged to separate recyclable materials from household garbage. Four years after the implementation of this program, in 2001, the amount of recyclable trash collection registered at 1.06 million tons, reflecting an increase of nearly 3 percent from the previous year. In 2003 this figure rose to 1.38 million tons.

In Taipei recycling trucks visit the city's neighborhoods three times a week to collect recyclable materials. Large home appliances and furniture that may be reused are collected by appointment. Nonrecyclable garbage must be disposed of in special blue bags. The purchase price of the bags includes a special fee for disposing of the garbage. These efforts have succeeded in reducing Taipei's daily trash production by a third as well as increasing its recyclable trash collection threefold.

NATURE CONSERVATION

The government of Taiwan has actively promoted nature conservation since the 1980s. In 1981 it enacted the Cultural Heritage Preservation Act, which mandates the creation of a system of nature reserves. In 1989 the Wildlife Conservation Act was enacted where 1,955 species of rare fauna were classified into three levels of protection—"endangered," "rare and valuable," and "requiring conservation measures."

FOREST RESERVES About 72 percent of the 4 million acres (1.6 million ha) of forestland in Taiwan are natural forests. Forest reserves are national forestlands recognized as possessing unique characteristics and their preservation is emphasized over land development.

Under a forest conservation program launched in 1965, the Forestry Bureau surveys and identifies different kinds of representative ecosystems, rare plants, and animals. It also drafts plans for long-term study and educational tourism within protected nature areas. The Forestry Bureau operates a network of hostels in forest areas that are more than a day's journey from any city and these hostels are open to the public for a fee, depending on the services available and the length of stay.

PROTECTION OF ENDANGERED SPECIES The Cultural Heritage Conservation Law prohibits hunting, fishing, collecting, logging, or other forms of destruction of designated rare and valuable animals and plants. Since 1982, 23 species of fauna and 11 species of flora have been identified by the Council of Agriculture as rare and valuable. Many of these plants and animals are endemic to Taiwan and include the Formosan black bear, the Mikado pheasant, the Taiwan pleione, and the Taiwan amentotaxus.

Wild birds gather in droves in the protected area of the Sihcao Wildlife Preserve.

53

TAIWANESE

TAIWAN IS ONE OF THE most densely populated places in the world, with an average density of 1,605 people per square mile (620 per square km). By comparison, the population density of the United States, according to the last census in 2000, is 79 people per square mile (30 per square km). Kao-hsiung, Taiwan's most populated urban area, has 25,464 people per square mile (9,827 per square km). Next comes Taipei City with 25,186 people per square mile (9,720 per square km) followed by T'ai-chung City with 1,580 people per square mile (610 per square km).

The 22.9 million people of Taiwan are essentially urban. In recent years the boundaries of urban areas have extended beyond the official limits of major cities, leading to the formation of large metropolitan areas that are now home to more than two-thirds, or 69 percent, of Taiwan's total population. Since industrial development took off in the 1960s, the number of rural residents has dwindled as more families leave their farms to work in industry. However, with the establishment of satellite towns and the progressive construction of basic infrastructure nationwide, the population influx to urban areas has decelerated.

THE CHINESE IN TAIWAN

The majority of people in Taiwan (about 98 percent) are Han Chinese, the dominant ethnic group of China. Han is the name commonly given to the Chinese people who originated from the central plains of China. Among the Han Chinese in Taiwan, there are substantial differences between native Taiwanese and mainlanders.

NATIVE TAIWANESE The native Taiwanese are those whose families arrived in Taiwan from the Chinese mainland before 1945. Few Chinese immigrants came to Taiwan during the Japanese colonial period. There is

Opposite: **A group of children celebrating Christmas. There are a variety of religions in Taiwan, and Christianity is one of them.**

After the 1949 exodus, Taiwan's people were isolated from the Chinese mainland as a result of the Taiwanese government's ban on traveling to the mainland. In 1987 this ban was lifted, and for the first time in 38 years, many people were able to travel to China to visit relatives whom they had not seen since 1949.

thus, in effect, a fifty-year gap between those who arrived before and after 1945, which makes it easy to understand the differences and distinctions between mainlanders and the native Taiwanese who make up 85 percent of the population and are mostly either Hakkas (HAH-kahs), or from the Fujian and Guangdong provinces.

The Hakkas originally came from Hunan province in China. For centuries they were a wandering people, and the name Hakka means "guest," suggesting temporary occupation. Within China many moved to Guangdong and Fujian provinces to escape the northern tribes that had invaded their home provinces; eventually many of them migrated to Taiwan. It is believed that Hakkas were among the first migrants to arrive from mainland China in the 12th century. Most of the Hakkas now live in northeastern Taiwan.

MAINLANDERS The mainlanders are so called because they are the immigrants who fled the mainland just before or soon after the Communist victory there in 1949. The term also applies to their descendants. When the 1.5 million mainlanders first arrived in Taiwan, their impact on society was great. Almost overnight the population of Taiwan swelled from 6 million to 7.5 million. The immigrants occupied many of the government and administrative positions in Taiwan and, in effect, controlled the government.

ETHNIC UNREST Relations between the native Taiwanese and the mainlanders have not always been easy. The 2-28 incident in 1947 was the worst and most violent expression of antagonism between the two groups. The native Taiwanese resented the fact that mainlanders, while accounting for less than 15 percent of the population, effectively controlled

THE 2-28 INCIDENT

A dark, unhappy incident occurred in Taiwan on February 27, 1947. On that day, customs officers caught a woman selling black market cigarettes in the street and tried to confiscate her goods. A scuffle broke out, and the woman was injured. When some Taiwanese tried to help her, a customs officer opened fire with his gun and a bystander was killed.

This single incident led to an angry backlash in Taiwan the next day as native Taiwanese protested all over the country against the customs officers' high-handed attitude. Violent demonstrations broke out, and the governor, Chen I, called for reinforcements from the mainland. The protests were ruthlessly put down, and thousands of native Taiwanese were arrested and executed, or simply disappeared. It is believed that between 18,000 to 28,000 people died as a result of the 2-28 incident, named after the riots that took place on February 28. Even today, it remains a bitter and painful reminder of the gulf between native Taiwanese and the mainlanders.

the government. This situation only began changing in the 1970s, when President Chiang Ching-kuo allowed more native Taiwanese to enter the political arena, and chose Lee Teng-hui, a native Taiwanese, to be vice president. When Lee became president in 1988 after Chiang's death, this was regarded as a momentous event in Taiwan's political history.

There remains some lingering resentment between the native Taiwanese and the mainlanders, who are sometimes thought to be arrogant. However, as many of the original mainlanders who came to Taiwan in 1949 are replaced by a new generation, greater assimilation between the two groups is occurring. Young Taiwanese pay little attention to ethnic differences, while increasing instances of intermarriage between mainlanders and the native Taiwanese have also helped to narrow the remaining gap between them.

THE ABORIGINES

Taiwan has approximately half a million aborigines, or *yuanzhu min* (YOO-an Ju min), meaning original people—the indigenous people of the island. They are believed to be of Austronesian stock, having arrived in Taiwan from regions as far away as Easter Island, Madagascar, and New Zealand. They currently make up less than 2 percent of the entire Taiwanese population.

There are currently 12 major indigenous tribes in Taiwan. They are the Ami, Atayal, Yami, Saisiyat, Paiwan, Bunun, Punuyumayan, Rukai, Tsou, Kavalan, Thao, and Truku. The Ami group is the largest of them, accounting for more than one-third of the indigenous population.

The aborigines are physically different from the Han Chinese in that they tend to have darker skin, bigger eyes, and sharper noses. Originally they lived in the plains, but with the arrival of the mainland Chinese over the centuries, they gradually retreated into the mountains. Their traditional occupations were farming, hunting, animal husbandry, and fishing. They are still involved in crafts such as weaving and metalwork.

Until the 20th century all of Taiwan's aborigines, except for the Yami, practiced headhunting. Although Chinese officials tried to suppress the practice, they were unsuccessful for a long time. It was only during the Japanese occupation of Taiwan that the custom of headhunting was completely abolished.

At Sun Moon Lake in the Central Range, the Formosan Aboriginal Culture Village houses a model re-creation of aboriginal villages representing each of the 12 tribes in Taiwan. Besides carrying on with their traditional lifestyle based on agriculture and hunting, some tribes have turned to making traditional crafts to attract tourist dollars.

AMI The largest aboriginal tribe in Taiwan is the Ami. They are found mainly in the eastern region of Taiwan from Hua-lien to T'ai-tung. The

Although many of Taiwan's aborigines today wear Western clothes, festivals and celebrations are still occasions to don traditional dress.

Ami have a matriarchal society in which the oldest woman in the family is the head of the household. The family name is carried on through the women, so children inherit their mother's name. When men get married, they traditionally move in with their wives' families.

Traditional Ami homes are thatched huts with wooden beams. Most houses are large communal dwellings because extended families live together. The Ami have a reverence for nature and worship gods of nature. They have many rites and ceremonies, the most important being the harvest festival held in July and August each year.

ATAYAL The Atayal people are distributed mainly over the northern parts of Taiwan. Some members live in the Taroko National Park. Like other aboriginals, the Atayal live on farming and hunting. Unlike the matriarchal Ami, Atayal men take their wives and children to live with their families. The Atayal religion is based on a belief in *utux* (OOH-tooks), or supernatural spirits and the spirits of the dead.

YAMI AND SAISIYAT They are the smallest tribal groups in Taiwan, each having about 4,200 people. The Yami peoples' homeland is Lan-yü, but many have left to live in Taiwan because of a lack of job opportunities on Lan-yü. They are mainly a fishing people who supplement their catch by breeding pigs and growing taro, sweet potato, yam, and millet. Traditionally, men and women have different roles—the men prepare the fields for cultivation,

An Ami woman. The Ami are mainly farmers. They are the only tribe to practise the craft of pottery making.

59

Atayal women continue to retain many of their traditions, including the art of weaving.

build boats, go fishing, build homes, weave baskets, and make pottery; the women tend to the crops and harvest them, take care of domestic affairs, and weave cloth. Being a fishing community, the Yami are famous for their beautifully carved and painted canoes.

The Yami also have a matriarchal system. Women can have trial marriages for one month; if a husband does not prove his worth by contributing to his wife's family, his wife can divorce him and look for a new husband.

The Saisiyat are mainly agriculturalists and foresters whose culture has been strongly influenced by their neighbors, the Atayal aborigines. Three or four households of the same name usually make up one Saisiyat settlement. A few neighboring settlements may join to form a village with shared farming land and amenities.

THE FUTURE FOR THE ABORIGINES

As Taiwan becomes increasingly more urbanized and industrialized, the rural and agricultural life of the aborigines no longer fits in with mainstream urban society. Many young aborigines leave their traditional homes to seek jobs in the towns and assimilate with the Taiwanese.

In 2002 the flow of indigenous people into the city numbered around 130,000—almost 30 percent of the indigenous population. There are fears that their culture and customs will be diluted and lost over time. However, the government's conscious effort to encourage cultural "pluralism," to allow room for the development and creation of conditions favorable for sustaining aboriginal heritage, reduces the intensity of such fears.

More concrete efforts to develop cultural pluralism can be seen through the establishment of the Council of Indigenous Peoples of the Executive Yuan—the agency responsible for indigenous affairs at the central government level—with corresponding organizations set up within the local governments of Taipei and Kao-hsiung.

In addition, young indigenous aborigines perceive education as a means of improving their lives. Special government scholarships are available to those students who are interested in studying overseas. The local and national political scene has also seen increased participation from Taiwan's indigenous people. Spelled out in Taiwan's Six-Year National Development Plan are efforts that will promote the economic independence of this community as well as encouragements to seek employment in local communities.

POPULATION POLICY

In the 1950s Taiwan embarked on a population control policy to contain the rising birthrate. Families were encouraged to have fewer children with the slogan, "Two is just right, one is not too few." The result was a marked reduction in population growth, with the birthrate falling from 5 percent in 1951 to 1 percent in 2003.

The success of this policy has created unforeseen problems—an aging population and too few babies—which will place a heavier burden on Taiwan's young and the future generations. About 7 percent of Taiwan's population is over 65, and this proportion is expected to reach 19 percent in the next 40 years. To rectify this imbalance, in 1992 the government introduced a revised slogan to its population policy: "Two is just right." The shift in population policy led to a slight increase in birthrates, recorded at 1.4 percent in 2000. This upsurge proved to be temporary, however, and the numbers fell back to 1 percent in 2002.

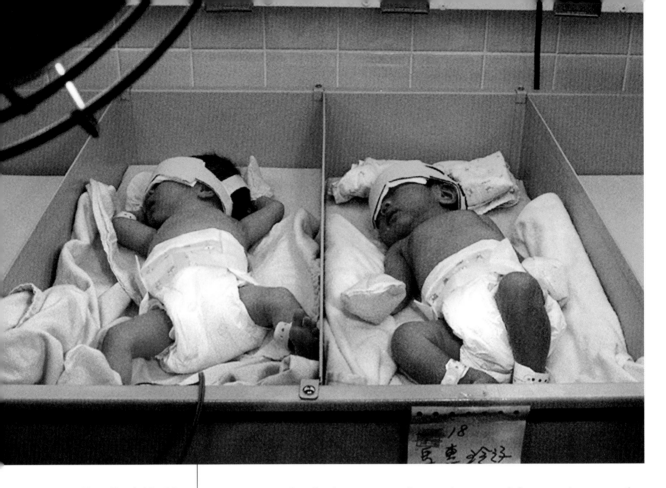

Longer periods of education, and a tendency to delay marriage are also some of the reasons why fewer women between the ages of 20 and 34 are having children—resulting in the low birthrates in Taiwan. Since 1984, the population replacement rate has stayed below 1 percent, dropping to as low as 0.6 percent in 2003.

Recent trends in Taiwan have shown a marked increase in the number of foreign marriages. In 2003 one in every three marriages involved a foreign partner, almost invariably the bride. Most foreign brides come from Southeast Asia, mainly Vietnam and mainland China.

TRADITIONAL DRESS

Apart from the traditional dress of the aborigines, clothes in Taiwan are the same as those worn in mainland China. On some occasions, women may wear the traditional *chi pao* (CHEE pow), a long, slim-fitting, knee- or ankle-length dress with a slit at each side and a high mandarin collar.

NAMES AND NAME CARDS

Chinese names are different from Western names in one important respect—the surname comes first. This practice is common in the countries of northeast Asia, including China, Japan, and Korea. So a girl whose name is Mei-ling and whose surname is Li will be called Li Mei-ling. However, if she happens to have a Christian name, it will precede her surname. If her Christian name is Mary, for instance, she will be known as Mary Li Mei-ling. Traditionally, the Chinese choice of names tends to follow notions of sexual roles. Girls' names are usually based on flowers or beautiful objects, and convey fragility and feminine values. Mei-ling, for example, means "beautiful flower." Boys' names tend to portray values such as courage and strength.

An interesting custom in Taiwan is the use of name cards. Just about everyone carries name cards, which are presented when people are introduced to each other. There is often a minor ceremony attached to presenting name cards—the person offering holds the card out with both hands and may bow slightly. The person receiving it reciprocates with both hands and a slight bow. Both sides of the card may be printed—one side with the name in Chinese characters and the other side in English.

The dress is usually made of a rich Chinese silk and has a beautiful floral print. It is often sleeveless or has short sleeves, although long sleeves are also possible. The *chang pao* (CHAHNG pow) is the traditional dress for men. It consists of three pieces—a black, waist-length jacket with a Mandarin collar and long, loose sleeves; a dark blue underskirt that extends to the knees and has slits at the sides; and long, black, loose-fitting trousers.

Both the *chi pao* and *chang pao* are modified forms of traditional Ching dynasty dress. It is becoming increasingly rare to find them in Taiwan's modern society. Both the young and old wear Western-style clothing on a daily basis, leaving traditional clothes to be worn only on special occasions. Even then, more women than men wear traditional clothes. At weddings, for instance, the bride usually changes from a Western-style dress into a *chi pao* at the wedding reception, but the groom continues to wear his Western-style suit. Among the wedding guests, it is usually the older people who wear traditional clothes.

LIFESTYLE

THE TAIWANESE LIFESTYLE has undergone a dramatic transformation in the past 40 years as a result of urbanization and industrialization. Economic prosperity has changed the face of modern Taiwan. Standards of living are far superior to what they were just one generation ago—in the 1960s, few families could afford consumer appliances such as televisions and even telephones. Just about every home in Taiwan now has its own television, refrigerator, washing machine, and telephone.

But in spite of rapid modernization and Taiwan's increasing exposure to Western trends, values, and ideas, the fundamental forces binding the family and society together remain rooted in Chinese tradition.

CONFUCIANISM

Confucian ethics are the single most important element in Taiwanese people's values and beliefs. Confucianism is the name given to the teachings of China's greatest teacher and philosopher. Although many of the practices associated with Confucianism have been mistakenly called a religion, in reality it is a code of conduct. Confucianism focuses on maintaining harmony in the world. Everyone is believed to have a particular place in their society and in the world, and if people respect preset rules of social behavior, social harmony will result.

Confucius prescribed a code of behavior for five specific categories of relationships—loyalty of a subject to a ruler, of a son to his father, of a younger brother to an elder brother, of a wife to a husband, and of one friend to another. This code was a set of rules that taught people about

Above: **Shop signboards advertising the numerous services available in the city crowd the space above a narrow road.**

Opposite: **Incense burning is an integral part of the ritual of worship in Chinese culture.**

Confucian priests conducting a ritual in one of the many Confucian temples in Taiwan.

"The Chinese people have shown the greatest loyalty to family and clan, with the result that in China there have been 'family-ism' and 'clan-ism' but no real nationalism."

—Dr. Sun Yat-sen

the sort of behavior required in each relationship. The respect and loyalty that are integral parts of each relationship are fundamental Confucian values aimed at strengthening social harmony. Confucianism is thus often called "a code of conduct, a guide to morality and good government." All aspects of Taiwanese and Chinese life are to some extent influenced by the teachings of Confucius.

Filial piety, called *hsiao* (SEE-ow), or respect and obedience to one's family elders, is one of the most important Confucian virtues. It operates as a strong force binding families together in Taiwan: increasing Westernization has not eroded this force.

THE IMPORTANCE OF FAMILY

The Confucian focus on group solidarity and harmony is best seen in the family model. The family is not only the most important unit of society in Taiwan, but it is also the strongest and most cohesive social unit.

CONFUCIUS—THE TEACHER OF ALL GENERATIONS

China's most famous teacher and philosopher, Kung Fu-tze (called Confucius), was born in mainland China in 551 B.C. during what is known as the Warring States period. This was a time of great anarchy and confusion in China as different warlords struggled for power.

Confucius's father died when he was very young, so he was brought up by his mother and was largely self-educated. He was very disturbed by the political and social chaos of those times and believed they were caused by corrupt officials who had abandoned the correct codes of conduct. Although Confucius tried to get a job in the civil service that would allow him to implement his ideas, he was not very successful. So he decided instead to travel around the country to spread his beliefs on the value of humanitarian behavior, loyalty to the family, and respect for authority. Two of his most important teachings focused on the concepts of *li* (lee), meaning ritual or etiquette, and *jen* (jehn), meaning kindness and benevolence to all human beings. He believed that if everyone practiced *jen*, the world would be a better place. According to Confucius, the ideal man should be a *chun tzu* (JUN-een-tzi), a perfect gentleman who lives according to his principles.

In those days education was available only to rich noblemen. Confucius defied tradition by opening a school that accepted all pupils regardless of wealth or status. Over a period of 40 years, he taught approximately 3,000 pupils from all backgrounds on the subjects of ritual, music, archery, driving chariots, history, and mathematics. Many of his teachings survive today in a collection called *The Analects of Confucius.*

Confucius died in 479 B.C., but his influence has not diminished. He is remembered and venerated in China and Taiwan as the Great Sage who established a code of conduct that forms the core of Chinese culture and lifestyle. His teachings have survived the test of time for 2,500 years. Every child in present-day Taiwan learns about Confucius's teachings. Every year on September 28 the entire island of Taiwan celebrates the birthday of this great teacher.

Children are brought up to respect the family structure and to understand that their primary duty is to the family. This ensures that filial piety is perpetuated and that families remain close-knit. Families also feature strongly in Taiwanese and Chinese society as a source of comfort and support in times of illness or trouble for individual members.

In the traditional family structure, extended families often live together, so that a single household may have as many as 10 to 50 members. It used to be very common for at least three generations to live together, with the grandparents, adult children, and grandchildren all residing under the same roof. At one time, having many children was considered to be a way of honoring the family ancestors. Before family planning became commonly practiced, couples sometimes had as many as eight to 10 children; as each of those children grew up and had their own large families, a single extended family could have up to 100 members.

Large extended families are no longer the norm in urban Taiwan, where living constraints have led to the increasing prevalence of nuclear families. In crowded and expensive cities, especially in Taipei, the cost of maintaining large households is just too much for the average family to bear. It is now common for sons and daughters to get their own apartments when they marry and start their own families. As such, aging parents sometimes live alone, although they often move in with their children once there are grandchildren. Family size is also shrinking, and most married couples nowadays tend to have only one or two children.

Until recently, Taiwan was a predominantly agricultural society. Women, as well as men, were workers, particularly in family farming. However, men were more likely to engage in trade and other forms of nonagricultural, waged labor. As more women now work outside of

Extended families of three or more generations are common in Taiwan. Even if they do not live together today, close ties are still maintained among family members.

family farming and are financially independent, their role in the family is rapidly changing. More women are resisting the traditional thinking that their place is confined to the home. The role of the head of the household has also been redefined in modern Taiwanese society. Fathers once had absolute authority in the family and made all the decisions, but today their sons and daughters also expect to have a say in family matters, mainly because they may be better educated than the father.

The role of grandparents has also changed. Previously, they were considered the guardians of wisdom in extended families, and their opinions were sought after and respected. As many of the elder generation now live apart from their children and grandchildren, they have less influence in guiding family members. The traditional Chinese concept of family harmony has, to some extent, been eroded by an urban lifestyle. Nonetheless, grandparents continue to play a big role in rearing children. Daycare, nannies and babysitters are rare in Taiwan because in most families grandparents are happy to take care of the youngsters when the parents are busy.

CHILDREN AND THE AGED

A major part of Taiwanese family life revolves around the children, and parents sometimes pamper them by giving in to their demands. Many traditional ideas about children remain. Sons are usually more cherished than daughters as they carry on the family name and perform the filial role of caring for elderly parents.

In the cities, the nuclear family is becoming the norm, and older people may see their children and grandchildren only during holidays.

69

The extent to which children are cherished in Taiwan can be seen in the Children's Welfare Law, instituted to protect children. Unborn children are protected in a clause that prohibits pregnant mothers from smoking, drinking, or consuming any drug or substance that could put an unborn child in danger. Parents are not allowed to leave children under the age of 6 unsupervised, and parents who deprive children of the compulsory nine years of education can face legal prosecution.

Heavily influenced by Confucian tradition, Taiwanese people tend to respect the elderly, who are believed to have acquired wisdom after a lifetime of experience. Filial piety also reinforces this respect, and most Taiwanese feel an obligation to look after their elderly parents and relatives.

THE FLAVOR OF HUMAN FEELING

A unique cultural characteristic of the Taiwanese is *ren ching wei* (rhen ching WAY). Loosely translated, this means "the flavor of human feeling." It is a concept difficult to define in words but is seen in the appreciation of social relationships and experiences. All experiences, whether good or bad, add to the flavor of human feeling and contribute to the pulse of the Taiwanese lifestyle.

GUAN HSI *AND KEEPING FACE*

Guan hsi (GWAHN see), or connections, refers to the relationships between people in an extended family, in business, and in social situations that

A loving grandmother tenderly cuddles her granddaughter. In both Chinese and Taiwanese societies, grandparents traditionally have an important role in help-ing to take care of their grandchildren.

A family enjoys leisure time together. Chinese culture places great importance on harmony within the extended family as well as in social relationships, so tact and diplomacy are an integral part of the Taiwanese lifestyle.

are often relied on to get things done. The person performing a favor can call on his or her *guan hsi* at any time for a favor in return. "Keeping face" or "saving face" is characteristic of Chinese society. Basically, it is the idea of upholding a person's prestige and dignity in society, and it is important to everyone, both rich and poor.

WEDDINGS

Although the Taiwanese lifestyle has, to some extent, been influenced by Western trends, weddings and funerals are occasions when Chinese customs, traditions, and values still prevail. Until two generations ago, many marriages in Taiwan were arranged by the couple's parents. Sometimes the bride and groom might not even have seen each other until the wedding. But with a more open and modern society, most people now choose their spouses. Nonetheless, parents still play some role in bringing young people together in the *hsiang chin* (SEE-ahng chin), a formal meeting when a young man and woman are introduced

Most bridal couples choose to wear Western-style dresses and outfits, although some of them will change into traditional clothes at some point during the wedding celebrations.

with the family members present. If they like each other, they begin to date.

When a couple decides to get engaged, their parents consult astrologers to determine whether the match is a good one and to choose an auspicious wedding date. To formalize the engagement, the fiancée is formally introduced to her prospective husband's family and serves them sweet tea. In return, she is given gifts of money in small red envelopes called *hung bao* (HOHNG bow). At the end of this ceremony, rings are exchanged, and there is a formal banquet attended by the whole family.

The wedding ceremony takes place at the favorable date and time chosen by the astrologer. The groom goes to the bride's house, where the couple has a farewell meal, symbolizing the last meal the bride takes in her familial home. Upon reaching the groom's house, the couple must first pay respects to the family ancestors by burning incense at the family altar. After the wedding ceremony, a banquet rounds off the celebrations. Family and friends bring gifts of money in *hung bao*. During the banquet they toast the couple and wish them happiness.

FUNERALS

Chinese death customs involve elaborate rituals prior to and during cremations or burials, but the rituals do not end there. The Taiwanese believe that a person becomes a spirit after death. Therefore, certain rites must be performed to cater to the needs of the deceased's spirit. Before the funeral, the family bows and kneels before the open coffin. They

A band provides musical accompaniment during funeral rites and the procession to the grave-yard. Before burial or cremation, the body of the deceased lies in an open coffin at home or in a funeral parlor. Friends of the family offer condolences and money to help with the funeral expenses, which can be very high.

wear white clothes made of rough cloth or burlap to show their grief. A seven-week mourning period is customary, at the end of which offerings are made to the deceased—sacrificial paper money, paper cars, paper clothes, paper houses, and other material goods are ritually burned in the belief that they will offer the departed an adequate lifestyle in the spirit world.

THE STATUS OF WOMEN

In traditional Chinese society, women were considered to be of a lower social status than men. Confucius taught that a woman's primary role was to serve her husband and family. The ideal qualities for women were passivity and submissiveness.

Women in modern Taiwanese society have made tremendous strides through higher education and better opportunities, and more Taiwanese women are working in the business, government, and education sectors than ever before.

Women have always worked in agriculture, and the small and medium-sized enterprises that were the mainstay of Taiwan's industrialization

A female biochemist working in a laboratory. Taiwanese women have made increasing forays into various professional work occupations.

usually employed all the adult members of a family, male and female. There was really never a period in Taiwan's history when large numbers of women did not have some form of employment, though these may not have been paid labor.

Although the constitution provides for equality of the sexes, in reality many traditional attitudes regarding women's place in society still persist, and women in Taiwan are a long way from being on an equal footing with men.

Many laws do not fully grant recognition of women's rights. In cases of divorce, for example, custody of the children is automatically given to the husband, and no alimony is granted to the wife. However, there is now a growing awareness of women's rights, thanks to the efforts of two women's organizations, the Awakening Foundation and the Warm Life Association. Both groups are campaigning for a change in divorce laws and more liberalized roles for men and women.

Divorce is very much a taboo subject in Taiwan. Thirty years ago it was almost unheard of, and although rare instances of divorce do take place now, it is still a subject that the Taiwanese feel uncomfortable discussing. Modern society is slowly coming to terms with the issue of divorce, but a stigma remains, more so for women than for men.

THE IMPORTANCE OF EDUCATION

Following the Confucian emphasis on learning and the traditional respect that the Chinese have for scholars, education has always been greatly valued in Taiwan. According to the Educational Budget Allocation and Management Act—passed by the legislative *yuan* in 2000—from 2002 onward, the education budget must equal at least 21.5 percent of the average of the previous three years. The government makes a concerted effort to ensure equal educational opportunities for all—children from low-income families receive free textbooks and financial aid.

Over the past decade the focus of Taiwan's educational system has been on the development of higher education. For the 2003 fiscal year the government spent 20.76 percent of its budget for educational purposes. Total educational expenditures (including both public and private sectors) of that year exceeded NT$634.85 billion (US$18.44 billion), or about 6.23 percent of the gross national product (GNP). Of these monies, 34.97 percent went to high schools and vocational schools, colleges, and universities, and 46.47 percent to the elementary and junior high schools of the compulsory education system.

Elementary education is compulsory for all children from age 6 to 12, and almost 100 percent of children in this age group attend school. At the end of July 2004 Taiwan had more than 2,600 elementary schools, with the vast majority being state-run schools. Elementary schoolchildren learn subjects such as language, science, arithmetic, civics, arts, music, and physical education.

Besides such conventional subjects as math or languages, children in Taiwanese schools are taught Confucian values of filial piety, patriotism, obedience to authority, and the importance of academic achievement.

Junior high school, which is part of the nine-year compulsory education program, lasts three years. Besides continuing with the learning of subjects taught in elementary schools, students also study a foreign language, for example English, and other subjects, such as mathematics, biology, chemistry, physics, and history. Those attending senior high school for three years have three main options upon graduation: move on to a university or college; attend a two-year junior college; or enroll in a four-year institute of technology after one year of work—provided that the candidates have passed the relevant qualifying examinations.

To gain admission at universities and colleges, students from senior high schools and vocational schools have to sit for a joint university entrance examination. Competition is very stiff. Among the courses offered in higher education are liberal arts, law, business, physical sciences, engineering and industrial management, life sciences, biological engineering, agriculture, medicine, and applied agricultural sciences. In the academic year of 2004–05 there were more than 142 universities and colleges in Taiwan.

As of 2006 Taiwan had a high literacy rate of 96.1 percent. Most illiterate people belong to the older generation. Some did not attend school because of disabilities. Special educational policies now cater to this segment of the population—special schools serve the needs of the physically and mentally challenged, and supplementary schools provide education for adults who missed out on schooling in their earlier years.

HEALTH CARE AND SOCIAL SERVICES

Since the 1960s, Taiwan's government has invested large sums in improving and expanding the island's health services. As a result, the Taiwanese have access to a comprehensive health-care system. The improvements

ACUPUNCTURE AND REFLEXOLOGY

Two Chinese medicinal practices that are well known all over the world are acupuncture and reflexology.

There is a story that during a battle many centuries ago in mainland China, a general was pierced in the head by an arrow. Amazingly, instead of causing him pain, the arrow cured him of a chronic pain from which he had been suffering. From this event, the Chinese are believed to have evolved the science of acupuncture. Acupuncture involves the insertion of needles into one or more of 365 specified points on the body. There are many stories of miracle cures. In fact, doctors in China and Taiwan have even performed major surgery on people using acupuncture instead of regular anesthesia. Although the patients were fully conscious during the operations, they felt absolutely no pain.

Reflexology involves massaging pressure points in the feet and hands to relieve ailments in other parts of the body. It is believed that the feet and hands contain pressure points linked to the body's internal organs through the circulatory, nervous, and energy systems. Stimulating these pressure points through massage stimulates the internal organs themselves.

in health have led to rising life expectancy among the population—from 53 years for men and 56 years for women in 1951 to 74 years for men and 80 years for women in 2005.

In the 1950s Taiwan's major health problems and causes of death among the population were gastroenteritis, pneumonia, and communicable diseases. But with improved health care, cancer and heart disease now register as the major causes of death, very much similar to the health patterns in advanced countries like the United States. In fact, some of Taiwan's main public health concerns today are pollution and industrial hazards. The growing aging population is also a cause for concern, as this puts a strain on the national health system.

RELIGION

RELIGION IN TAIWAN is a combination of many beliefs. Most people do not follow just one religion but identify with two or more. Of the major world religions, Buddhism has the strongest influence in Taiwan, but Buddhist beliefs and practices also merge to a large extent with folk beliefs and other Chinese religions, such as Taoism.

Although many people in Taiwan may not belong to any religious group nor have a formal place of worship, they still subscribe to traditional beliefs. Most homes have family altars and shrines where they perform the rites of ancestral worship: incense is burned, and offerings are made to the gods.

BUDDHISM

Buddhism came to China from India in the first century A.D. but only became established as a major religion during the Sui (A.D. 581–618) and Tang (A.D. 618–907) dynasties. In the late Ming (1368–1644) and early Qing (1644–1911) dynasties, immigrants from the mainland took the religion to Taiwan. After Koxinga drove the Dutch out of Taiwan in 1662, more Buddhist monks came to the island. In the 17th and 18th centuries a number of Buddhist temples were built, some of which still survive.

Although Buddhism is considered a religion in China and Taiwan, it is in essence more a philosophy of life. It was founded in India in the sixth century B.C. by Siddhartha Gautama, who was disillusioned by the misery and injustice he observed in the world, and who attained spiritual enlightenment after meditating for many years. The name Buddha means "The Enlightened One." Buddha taught that craving and desire were the source of human suffering and that meditation and the search for truth

Above: **Lungshan temple in Taipei has impressive murals and intricately carved pillars. The temple is dedicated to Kuan Yin, the goddess of mercy, worshipped by Buddhists and Taoists alike.**

Opposite: **A giant statue of Buddha.**

Buddhist monks at prayer. Buddhism teaches its followers to help deliver all beings from worldly desire and suffering.

could lead to spiritual enlightenment. Buddhism worldwide is practiced in two forms—Mahayana Buddhism preaches universal salvation through faith and devotion to Buddha; Hinayana Buddhism is more concerned with salvation through contemplation and self-purification.

Buddhism in Taiwan has undergone a revival in the past 10 years. The Buddhist clergy has begun to play a more active role in preaching the religion and in promoting charity work and social causes, for example, by subsidizing medical services and giving financial support to homes for the elderly. The Buddhist Compassion Relief Tzu Chi Foundation is the largest and best-known charitable organization in Taiwan. It has sent emergency relief to disasters in many countries, including those affected by the tsunami that devastated parts of Southeast Asia in December 2004. The number of Buddhists in Taiwan has grown sixfold from 800,000 in 1983 to more than five million in 2005. Two major Buddhist sects are the Pure Land and the Zen sects.

Fokuangshan (meaning "Light of Buddha Mountain") Monastery near Kao-hsiung is a major center of Mahayana Buddhist studies in Taiwan, attracting pilgrims from Asia. The place is also home to Taiwan's largest Buddhist temple complex. Its 82-foot (25-m) gold statue of Buddha is the tallest in Taiwan.

TAOISM

Taoism originated in China 2,500 years ago, at
about the same time that Confucius taught his
ideas. Its founder is Lao Tzu (meaning "Old
One"), whose teachings are contained in a
book, the *Tao Teh Ching* (TAH-oo der ching).
Taoism advocates living a life of simplicity
and passivity by following *tao*, meaning the
guiding path that leads to immortality. With the
spread of Taoism, Lao Tzu achieved the status
of an immortal being and was later regarded
as a Taoist god. Other people who lived in
harmony with nature were also believed to
have become immortal and were worshipped
as gods.

Taoist priests pray to
ward off evil spirits at
Taipei's Hua Hsi night
market.

As with Buddhism, Taoism was taken to Taiwan by immigrants from the
mainland. To some extent, it has merged with Buddhist and folk beliefs
in Taiwan. Unlike Buddhist temples, which maintain a simple austerity,
Taoist temples in Taiwan are the sites of elaborate rites where Taoist
priests offer thanksgiving prayers to the gods and pray for prosperity and
happiness. Since Taoists believe in supernatural spirits, Taoist priests are
often called upon to exorcise evil spirits and bless homes and offices.

FOLK RELIGION

Folk religion, too, arrived in Taiwan with the early immigrants. In common
with the Chinese characteristic of merging beliefs and philosophies,
Taiwanese folk religion absorbed many beliefs from Buddhism and

Taoism. It also has a number of gods and goddesses in common with Buddhism and Taoism, including Kuan Yin, the goddess of mercy.

The supreme deity in folk religion is the god of heaven. Other gods include Matsu—goddess of the sea—the house god, and the earth god. Many gods were once mortal men and women who, after their deaths, were elevated to the status of gods because they had achieved some fame or honor during their lives. For instance, Kuankung was a faithful friend of the emperor in the third century A.D. His integrity and loyalty earned him the status of a folk god.

Religious devotees carry their gods in litters suspended from poles to the principal temple of the goddess Matsu in Beigang, south of Taipei.

SPIRIT WORLD OF THE ABORIGINES

The aborigines of Taiwan believe in spirits that live in inanimate objects, such as stones and trees. These are said to be the spirits of people who have died. After death they were liberated from their human bodies to dwell in the spirit world. A great part of aboriginal religious ritual involves appeasing these spirits as they can unleash destruction on humanity

THE LIVING AND THE DEAD

A crucial part of Chinese religious belief focuses on the philosophy that people are rewarded for good deeds by becoming gods and entering heaven after they die. Those guilty of evil deeds are punished by being transformed into ghosts and sent to hell. Both gods and ghosts must be appeased and worshipped by the living. Departed ancestors are also believed to have power. As angry ancestors can cause bad luck, their descendants make offerings to keep their spirits happy.

KUAN YIN, GODDESS OF MERCY

One of the most important deities in the Chinese pantheon is Kuan Yin, who was once a young woman called Miau Chan. According to legend, Miau Chan was a very kind and compassionate girl. When she grew up, her father wanted her to get married, but Miau Chan chose to enter a nunnery. When her father tried to discourage her from this by making sure she had to do all the most difficult chores, Miau Chan became even more determined to devote her life to religion. Finally her father had her killed.

Miau Chan's goodness of spirit was so strong that the gods sent her back to earth, where she saved her father from a fatal illness by sacrificing herself. When her father discovered this, he was overcome with remorse, gave up all his worldly goods, and became a Buddhist.

After this Miau Chan became known as Kuan Yin, or "One who Sees and Hears the Cry of the Human World." She symbolizes the greatest loving kindness and compassion. Interestingly, Kuan Yin is a goddess for both Buddhists and Taoists. She is especially worshipped by women who want to have children and by people seeking forgiveness for wrongdoings.

In Taiwan over 500 temples are dedicated to Kuan Yin. Among the most famous is the Lungshan temple in Taipei, dating back to the 18th century. Images of Kuan Yin usually show the goddess holding a vase containing the dew of compassion. According to legend, a sprinkling of this dew can heal illnesses miraculously.

when any wrongdoing is committed. On the other hand, when people live according to the rules of society, the spirits help them and grant them their wishes.

The Ami believe that, once upon a time, a male god was born from the splitting of mountains and a female god was born from a tree after a flood in a bamboo forest. These two gods are believed to be the ancestors of human beings. The Saisiyat believe that in ancient times there was a flood that drowned everyone. The only survivor was cut into pieces by the gods and thrown into the sea. From these pieces human beings were born again.

OTHER RELIGIONS

I-kuan Tao is the third most popular religion in Taiwan. Literally meaning "The Religion of One Unity," I-kuan Tao draws not only on traditional Chinese teachings but also from major religions, such as Buddhism, Taoism, Christianity, Islam, Judaism, and Hinduism. It preaches that, by uncovering

a single set of universal truths inherent in these major religions, people can live in peace and harmony.

Christianity came to Taiwan in the 16th century with the arrival of the Europeans. The Dutch introduced Protestantism, and the Spanish priests spread Roman Catholicism. In 2002 Taiwan had about 605,000 Protestants and 298,000 Catholics. The country's Muslim community is 53,000 strong. Some of these Muslims are descendants of soldiers who came to Taiwan as part of Koxinga's army, while others came from northern China in 1949, after the Communist takeover of the mainland.

Among the unique Chinese religions found in Taiwan are Tien Te Chiao and Li-ism. Tien Te Chiao is a religion that combines elements from Confucianism, Taoism, Buddhism, Christianity, and Islam. Li-ism combines the worship of Kuan Yin with Confucian, Buddhist, and Taoist principles. Both religions originated in mainland China. Unlike them, Hsuan Yuan Chiao was founded in Taiwan in 1957. It aims to revive Chinese nationalism and unify religious beliefs among the people.

MATSU—GODDESS OF THE SEA

Matsu was born in A.D. 960 in the Fujian province on mainland China. She was believed to have supernatural powers. One day, Matsu's father and brother were sailing homeward when a typhoon struck and sank their boat. At that time, Matsu was at home taking a nap, and in her sleep she dreamed that her father and brother were drowning. In her dream she used her supernatural powers to hold on to her father and brother, but when she heard her mother's voice calling out to her, she accidentally let go of her father, and he was swept away. When Matsu woke up, she found that her dream had been prophetic. Her mother broke the sad news that her father had been lost at sea but that her brother was safe. Matsu was so overcome with grief that she ran straight into the sea and disappeared. Three days later, she miraculously rose from the sea carrying her father's body. Legend says that after performing this miracle, Matsu ascended into heaven accompanied by angels, where she became a goddess.

During the Sung dynasty, Emperor Kang Hsi gave Matsu the supreme title of Empress of

Heaven. Temples consecrated to Matsu can be found all over Taiwan. The oldest Matsu temple in the P'eng-hu islands was built in 1573. The most famous is the temple at Pei-kan, where Matsu's birthday celebration on the 23rd day of the third lunar month draws hundreds of thousands of worshippers. During this event an image of the goddess is paraded around the island in an ornate palanquin, accompanied by bands playing traditional music and pilgrims carrying banners and offering money and incense to the goddess. There is a performance of a Taiwanese opera and lion dances, and a banquet is laid out for the pilgrims. In 1987 Matsu's followers celebrated the 1,000th anniversary of her ascent into heaven with great pomp and ceremony.

Among the people of the fishing community of Taiwan, Matsu is especially venerated as the goddess of the sea and the protector of sailors. Special prayers are offered to her each time they set out to sea, and thanksgiving prayers are offered again when they return safely.

LANGUAGE

THE NATIONAL LANGUAGE of the Republic of China on Taiwan is Mandarin, also known as *kuo yu* (GWOH ewe-ee), meaning "national language." It is one of the major branches of the Sino-Tibetan family of languages and is characterized by the use of tones to distinguish between the meanings of words and the fact that it is a monosyllabic language—each syllable has a different meaning. Mandarin is the only major writing system in the world that has continued its pictograph-based development without interruption until modern times.

THE OFFICIAL AND NATIONAL LANGUAGE

The origins of Mandarin as the national language of China can be traced to the Manchu Qing dynasty. For many centuries China's rulers faced a linguistic problem: in this vast land, people from different regions spoke many languages and dialects. In the 17th century Qing dynasty officials encouraged the spread of the Peking dialect, which was the language used by government officials, called mandarins. Their success was limited.

In 1913, after the overthrow of the Manchu and the founding of the Republic of China, the government established a national standard of pronunciation based on the Peking dialect, with the aim of promoting a national language for China. Since then, Mandarin has been the national language of both the Republic of China on Taiwan and the People's Republic of China on the mainland.

Although Mandarin is the national tongue of the Taiwanese, its usage varies among the different groups of people. Mainlanders speak Mandarin most of the time. Among the native Taiwanese, who form about 85 percent of the population, Mandarin is spoken in offices and shops but not necessarily at home. About half of the native Taiwanese speak other Chinese dialects with their families. Many of the older generation

The Chinese civilization was the first in the world to invent paper and printing. Recorded history shows that paper was first used in China in A.D. 105 and that printing was invented between 1041 and 1048, some 300 years before it was first used in Europe.

Opposite: **A man writing in calligraphy—an ancient Chinese art.**

of native Taiwanese may not speak Mandarin at all because they grew up during the Japanese occupation, when Japanese was taught in schools. Geographical locations also play a part. Young people living or working in the northern parts of Taiwan typically speak Mandarin with their friends, whereas those in the southern areas tend to speak a mixture of Taiwanese and Mandarin.

Taiwanese Mandarin has been influenced by the dialects spoken on the island, especially the Fujian dialect. In fact, some Fujian words that have crept into Taiwanese Mandarin are so common, even the mainlanders use them.

MANDARIN ACROSS THE TAIWAN STRAIT

Although Mandarin is the official language on both sides of the Taiwan Strait, the Republic of China on Taiwan calls it *kuo yu*, whereas the People's Republic of China on the mainland refers to it as *putonghua* (POO-tohng-hwa), meaning common language. Another area in which Mandarin differs between mainland China and Taiwan is in its romanized

form. This is a system of writing a language using the English alphabet, rather than a language's traditional characters. Mainland China uses the pinyin system of romanization, but Taiwan uses a different system—Tongyong pinyin. It was officially adopted in 2002, replacing the now defunct, older Wade-Giles system.

Pinyin is harder for non-Chinese speakers to learn, especially with regard to consonants. Syllables starting with the letters *x, q,* and *c* are the trickiest as they are pronounced more like *s, j,* and *ch,* respectively.

COMING TO GRIPS WITH MANDARIN

The Chinese language is said to be one of the most complex languages in the world to learn. Not only are the sounds of the words difficult for a non-Chinese speaker to master, but writing it is an even more demanding task. Mandarin is a monosyllabic language, and this means that each syllable as pronounced has a unique meaning. Words may be made up of either one or more syllables. Considering that there are

LEARNING MANDARIN IN TAIWAN

The government of Taiwan places great importance on language education and in promoting a standard written style. People from all over the world can enroll in Taiwan's numerous Mandarin training centers to study the Chinese language in its original form.

about 400 syllables in the Chinese language, coming to grips with the full range of sounds can be daunting. Another characteristic of Mandarin is that it is a tonal language, in which there are several ways to pronounce each syllable. In fact, changing the tone of a particular character changes the meaning of that character, as in the examples below.

The four tones are:

Constant (first tone), as in mā (mother)

Rising (second tone), as in má (hemp)

Falling and rising (third tone), as in mǎ (horse)

Falling (fourth tone), as in mà (scold)

The rules of writing Chinese characters are drilled into children at an early age; every stroke of a character is written in a specific direction and the strokes have to be written in the correct sequence.

These four tonal variances add to the complexity of pronouncing Mandarin words. As each syllable can be pronounced in four ways, there are over 1,200 different syllables!

The language is structured on the subject-verb-object order that is similar to English. However, there are no past or present tenses, singular or plural configurations, or other grammatical rules. Writing in Chinese characters requires a great deal of memory work. The language is made up of about 50,000 characters, although, to read a Chinese newspaper, the average person need know only about 2,000 characters.

DIALECTS

The two most widely spoken dialects are the Fujian and Hakka dialects. Each is a form of the Chinese language peculiar to certain areas in China. The Fujian dialect comes from Fujian Province on the mainland. It is more commonly spoken in the southern part of Taiwan and in parts of the western coastal region that have historically absorbed immigrants from Fujian. Hakka originated from Hunan province on the mainland and is widely spoken in Taiwan's Hsin-chu, P'ing-tung, Miao-li, and T'ao-yüan counties, which have a sizable Hakka population.

In the 1960s and 1970s Taiwan's official language policy was to place greater emphasis on Mandarin rather than the Chinese dialects. Now that Mandarin is firmly entrenched as the national language, there is greater interest among the people in learning dialects. This revived interest over the past few years has resulted in the greater usage of dialects in the media. Since the late 1980s, existing television and radio programs in the Fujian and Hakka dialects have been expanded, and new programs have been introduced.

WRITTEN CHINESE

Many Chinese dialects are so far removed from each other that any spoken communication is a hit-or-miss affair. Fortunately, there is a saving unifier in the written form of the language: all Chinese characters are written in exactly the same way regardless of dialect. So even if a government official from Peking is unable to communicate orally with someone from Fujian or Hunan province, they can communicate in writing. Chinese writing is based on ideograms—this means that each character is actually a pictorial representation of the idea being expressed. For instance, the characters

A street billboard advertising houses for sale in Chinese characters. In Taiwan, standard Chinese characters are used, instead of the simplified form used in mainland China and most other countries in the world.

Though many languages from ancient civilizations went through stages where they were written in pictorial form, the Chinese written language is unique in being the only major writing system in the world to continue using a pictorial form for over 3,000 years.

for woman, wood, and mountain in the illustration below are really simplified line drawings of the object.

Since 1964 the written form of Chinese in Taiwan and mainland China has been shaped along different paths. Believing that standard Chinese characters were too complex for the average person to master, the Chinese Communists introduced a simplified form of Chinese characters called *jiantidz* (JIAN ti tze). Taiwan, on the other hand, still retains the classical form of characters, called *fantidz* (FAHN ti tze).

CALLIGRAPHY

Calligraphy, or the art of writing, has been an important part of Chinese linguistic and artistic history for over 2,000 years. Because Chinese characters lend themselves to artistic interpretation, calligraphy is considered a cultural refinement. To a calligrapher a dot, for example,

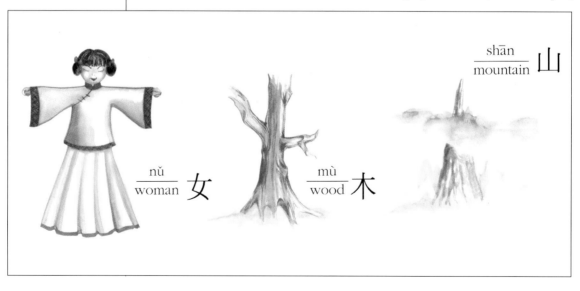

shān / mountain 山

nǔ / woman 女

mù / wood 木

is full of life, and a line may burst with energy. Like the branch of a tree or a thick vine, there is logic to the form and behavior of each stroke.

Many calligraphic works are written on scrolls that are often hung in homes, offices, and shops and at monuments. These contain fragments of poems or the sayings of famous people. Different writing styles have evolved over the centuries, including the seal script, official script, regular script, running script, and cursive script.

The "four treasures of study" essential to calligraphy are the brush pen, paper, ink stick, and inkstone. These are the tools with which Chinese characters are written in the traditional way. Brush pens are made from soft, fine, animal hair and date back 3,000 years. The earliest form of calligraphy (16th–11th centuries B.C.) was written on stones, tortoise shells, animal hides, and bones. Ever since the Chinese invented paper during the Eastern Han dynasty (A.D. 25–220), calligraphy has been written on paper. Today, calligraphy is an important subject taught in schools in Taiwan.

Practitioners of the art of Chinese calligraphy make sure that the ink, which must be black Chinese ink, is of the right consistency and the brush has the right contour. When wet, the brush takes on the shape of the flame of a candle—wide in the middle, where it is packed with bristles, but tapered to a fine point at the tip, where there are only a few of the longest hairs. This makes it possible to draw an extremely fine line.

OTHER LANGUAGES

Although English is taught in junior high schools, it is not widely spoken in Taiwan. Many of those who do speak English are not proficient in it, although they are generally better at written English. A legacy of Japan's 50-year occupation of Taiwan still lives on, with many of the older generation conversant with Japanese.

A bilingual sign at K'en-ting National Park. Tourism is a thriving industry in Taiwan, and signs in popular tourist sites cater to those who understand English.

Taiwan's aboriginal languages used to exist only in spoken form. Consequently, Taiwan's aborigines possess a rich oral tradition, as seen in the transmission of culture, legends, and beliefs by word of mouth. Recently, however, aboriginal languages were transliterated with the publication of the first aboriginal languages textbook series in 2000. The aboriginal languages have absolutely no similarity to any of the Chinese languages. In fact, they have more in common with the languages of Southeast Asia, especially the Malay and Filipino languages, which further reinforces the aborigines' ethnic link with the Malay-Polynesian peoples of Southeast Asia.

Today most aborigines speak Mandarin, and some of them speak the Fujian dialect. Unfortunately, as many of the younger generation of aborigines move away from their ancestral villages to live in towns, their links with their indigenous cultures and languages are weakening. This has raised the concern that some aboriginal languages and traditions are at risk of being slowly forgotten.

At various cultural performances by aboriginal tribes in places such as Hua-lien, visitors can still appreciate their hauntingly beautiful, melodious ancestral chants.

NEWSPAPERS

Not long ago, Taiwan's newspapers were subject to a very restrictive policy that effectively imposed censorship. From the early 1950s until 1988 the KMT did not allow any new newspaper to publish and even restricted the number of pages in each issue. In 1955 newspapers were allowed to run eight pages of news only; that number was increased to 12 in 1974 and to 32 (or even 40) pages at a later stage. In 1988 this restrictive policy was finally lifted, and as a result, many new newspapers have since been published. Indeed, Taiwan's respect for press freedom was recognized in 2005 in a finding by Freedom House.

In 2004 Taiwan had more than 3,000 newspapers, including 30 national newspapers and several hundred local papers. In 2003 the *Liberty Times* was the Chinese-language paper with the widest circulation, followed by *China Times* and *United Daily News*. The *Liberty Times* also publishes a U.S. edition through its Los Angeles branch office. The three main English-language newspapers in Taiwan are the *China Post*, the *Taiwan News*, and the *Taipei Times*.

CHINESE IDIOMS

Chinese is a concise language. What is said with four or five characters may require 10 or more English words to express. Many Chinese idioms put a point across succinctly and defy a direct translation into English in the same number of words. *Saiwen shi ma* (SAI-wen shi mah), literally "old Sai loses his horse," comes from the story of a man who, facing great hardship, claims to be calm even when his friends bemoan his misfortune. The saying is used to express a lack of concern when things do not go right. *Siow ti ta chuo* (see-ow ti DAH zwoh) literally means to write a long composition on a trivial topic, or to make mountains out of molehills. *Yin shui si yuan* (yin SHWAY si yoo-en), or "when you drink water, consider its source," means one must always bear in mind how the past has contributed to the present.

"A Chinese proverb contains a definite message or philosophy of life, whereas a Chinese idiom has a wider application. It could either have a moral intent or be an adept turn of phrase, a cogent expression with no deeper meaning. If an idiom delivers a wise thought or saying, it is in fact a proverb."

—*Tan Huay Peng,*
Chinese Idioms, Vol.1

ARTS

TAIWAN'S ARTS ARE VERY MUCH a part of the island's Chinese cultural legacy. With its rich, artistic heritage, Taiwan has a wide variety of art forms, from painting, carving, and calligraphy, to folk arts such as puppetry and Taiwanese opera. Taiwanese opera was a popular form of entertainment in the early 20th century.

FINE ARTS

In the mainstream of Chinese fine arts are calligraphy and painting. Traditional Chinese painting uses ink and watercolors rather than oil-based paints. Landscapes and scenes from nature, such as animals and trees, are the most popular subjects, but many modern painters are experimenting with new artistic forms and Western-influenced artistic media.

Carving in stone, wood, or bamboo is a respected craft. Stone carvings are usually found in temples. Just about every temple has a pair of carved stone lions at the entrance, and carvings of dragons decorate the columns of temples. Wood carvings, both miniature and large, are generally made of sandalwood or camphor wood. One of Taiwan's most famous contemporary artists and sculptors is Ju Ming. He has won international awards for his dramatic sculptures that give traditional Chinese subjects a modern look.

Chinese pottery and porcelain have been famous around the world since the Ming dynasty. Taiwan continues to produce the traditional blue and white ceramics for which Chinese potters are famous, as well as modern designs.

Above: **Dancing dragons symbolize the vigor and power of the gods. The theme of dancing dragons flanking the "celestial pearl" is thus the most common motif for temple buildings. These roof ornaments are believed to ward off evil influences and bring beneficial forces.**

Opposite: **A craftsman working intently on a detailed wood carving, surrounded by the tools of his trade.**

97

Rice-dough sculptures, shaped like ancient Chinese warriors, look almost too good to eat.

FOLK ARTS

Taiwan's diverse folk arts are part of its traditional culture. Many of the crafts evolved to celebrate the agricultural seasons, festivals, and major days in people's lives, such as birthdays, marriages, and deaths.

Paper cutting is one of the oldest folk arts. Red paper cutouts are pasted onto walls and windows to give homes a festive look. Knotting, or macramé, is used to make jewelry or wall hangings. During the Qing dynasty (1644–1911) silk macramé decorated clothing, fans, ceremonial flutes, window shades, jade scepters, and many other items. One traditional craft of the Hakka people is the making of oilpaper umbrellas. The Hakkas in the town of Meinung in southern Taiwan are well known for this specialty.

Just about every festive event in Taiwan features a dazzling display of lion and dragon dances, the origins of which can be traced back to ancient China. Dragons, in particular, symbolize power and good fortune. Lion dances are performed in religious ceremonies and for entertainment. The dance is performed by two people. One carries the lion's head and leads the dance while the other plays the lion's body. The performers dance

"Chinese artists put the eyes in last when they painted the dragon, for this brought the formidable creature to life."

—Dennis Bloodworth, An Eye for the Dragon

98

A traveling puppet theater brings this ancient folk art to the streets of Taiwan's cities.

to the loud and stirring rhythm of drums, gongs, and cymbals. Another folk art that is a favorite with children is that of candy and rice-dough sculptures. Candies made of sugar and rice dough are molded into colorful animal and human shapes and sprinkled with sugar. The skill and detail that go into creating them qualify them as folk art.

Taiwan's puppet theater has three forms—hand puppets, shadow puppets, and marionettes. These used to be an important part of many festivals and religious occasions but are now less popular among the people. The plots of puppet shows are usually based on myths, folk stories, and historical events. Some of these shows are broadcast on television.

There has been increasing concern in Taiwan that modern and Western influences may affect its folk art heritage. The annual four-day Lu-kang Folk Arts Festival aims to preserve Taiwan's unique art forms by promoting greater appreciation of them. Among the arts exhibited at the festival are lantern making, top spinning, candy and dough sculpting, paper cutting and folding, kite flying, carving, and puppetry. Dragon and lion dances, stilt walking, and music and dance performances keep audiences entertained and add to the festive atmosphere.

MUSICAL TRADITION

Taiwan's musical tradition falls into two categories—folk music, called *pei kuan* (BAY gwahn), and classical music. The folk music tradition has always been more popular in Taiwan. Most songs are sung in Mandarin, although dialects have been used increasingly in the past few decades. Most *pei kuan* performers are men, and each troupe usually has three to five, or even 10, performers.

Chinese classical music is the most ancient musical style in all of Chinese society. Taiwan has three professional orchestras that perform classical music—the Taipei Municipal Orchestra, the Experimental Chinese Orchestra of the National Taiwan Academy of Arts, and the Chinese Music Orchestra of the Broadcasting Corporation of China. There are also over 200 amateur and school orchestras. Many elementary, junior high, and senior high schools have classes teaching the use of traditional Chinese musical instruments.

Traditional musical instruments fall into four basic categories—those that can be blown, bowed, plucked, or struck. These include the *erhu* (ER-hoo), a two-stringed violin, the *yue chin* (YOO-eh chin), a four-stringed banjo, the *kucheng* (KOO-chuhng), a zither, and the *pipa* (PEE-pah), a four-stringed lute. Other traditional instruments, such as trumpets and gongs, are used mainly in religious ceremonies in temples and at

Members of a Chinese orchestra rehearsing before a performance in a music concert hall. The instrument shown is the *kehu* (KUH-hoo). The music produced on the *kehu* is so like that of a cello that some smaller orchestras use the cello in its place.

funerals. Sadly, interest in traditional Chinese music has suffered a decline as more people of present-day Taiwan prefer listening to contemporary pop and rock music.

TAIWANESE OPERA

Taiwanese opera is an offshoot of Peking opera, the most famous of Chinese dramatic forms. It is performed in the Fujian dialect and was taken to Taiwan by the early immigrants. The opera owes its popularity

Taiwanese opera is distinctive in its use of elaborate makeup, heavily embroidered costumes, stylized acting that takes years to master, and the actors' artificially high-pitched voices in both the dialogue and the songs.

Most operas tell stories of great historical events or folklore. A typical opera performance has dramatic swordfights between rivals, lovers' meetings, family disputes, and scenes of heartbreak and heroism.

to the artistic flowering that took place in mainland China in the Tang dynasty (A.D. 618–907), and certain Tang emperors are considered "the honorary fathers of Chinese opera" for their support of opera.

Most Taiwanese operas are performed in the open air on a simple stage with only a backdrop. Hardly any props are used because the performers' costumes and gestures and the music are so pictorial in themselves. Traditionally, the women's roles were played by men, but women now perform in modern operas. Each character has distinguishable costumes and fantastic facial makeup so that the audience can tell at a glance whom each player represents. Costumes worn in operas are based on those of the Ming dynasty over 400 years ago.

Facial makeup in Taiwanese opera, an art in itself, is an outward representation of a character's personality. The origins of this form of makeup go back almost 1,500 years. In the sixth century A.D., Prince Lan-ling of the Northern Wei kingdom tried to make himself look more fearsome in battle by painting an aggressive mask on his face. The strategy worked, and his enemies were so intimidated that they lost the battle, even though they had superior forces. Later, in the Tang dynasty, facial makeup was used in opera performances.

TAIWAN'S MOVIES

Taiwan has been actively producing movies since the 1960s. Many of the films cater to popular tastes and feature martial arts and sword fights. Taiwanese art films have won international acclaim since the 1980s. Among the award-winners at international film festivals are Taiwan-born Ang Lee's movies: *The Wedding Banquet; Crouching Tiger, Hidden Dragon;* and *Eat Drink Man Woman.* In 2006 Ang Lee won the Best Director Oscar for *Brokeback Mountain.* Other award-winning Taiwanese films include Hou Hsiao-hsien's *Cities of Sadness* and Edward Yang's *A Brighter Summer's Day.*

Today, different colors are used to symbolize different personalities. For instance, red indicates good character, white is for craftiness, blue represents bravery, black is for honesty, yellow signifies intelligence, brown suggests a strong personality, green is for ghosts or demons, and gold is for gods or good spirits.

Flowing, graceful movements characterize this folk dance.

CHINESE DANCE

In ancient times, music and dance were purely for rituals. With the passage of time, however, their function evolved into one of entertainment. Traditional Chinese dance has been divided into civilian and military dances for almost 3,000 years. Civilian dance has more free-flowing movements. Military dancers traditionally perform in large groups with coordinated movements.

A famous traditional dance in Taiwan is the Eight Rows Dance performed in temples every year during Confucius's birthday celebrations. Sixty-four young boys dressed in yellow robes are arranged in eight rows. Carrying pheasant tails and red batons, the boys bow, turn, and kneel in performing this stately dance that has remained unchanged since the Sung dynasty (A.D. 960–1279).

Taiwan is experiencing a revival of interest in dance, especially those with techniques that combine traditional and modern dance elements. Among the troupes that have won acclaim for their blending of Chinese dance techniques with modern dance choreography are the Cloud Gate Dance Troupe and the new Classical Dance Troupe.

ARCHITECTURAL STYLES IN TAIWAN

Because traditional Chinese society had large, extended families living together, typical Taiwanese homes were often big, rambling compounds that could house up to 50 family members. Most such homes consisted of one large central building with several wings or smaller buildings attached to it. The head of the family lived in the largest building, where the ancestral hall was also located. The hall held the family altar and portraits of deceased ancestors. The entire house, with its attached wings, was surrounded by a walled enclosure. Courtyards were important features of those homes because this was where the household chores were done. Another characteristic of this time-honored architecture is that buildings usually faced south. One possible reason for that could have been to avoid the harsh winds that blew down from the north.

A distinctive feature of Chinese architecture can be seen in the shape of roofs. In imperial China a person's social status was reflected in the roof of his home, and imperial court officials regulated the types of roofs people could build. Originally, only temples and government officials were allowed to have swallowtail roofs, where the ends of the roofs curved upward like a swallow's tail. Many wealthy families in Taiwan chose not to observe this mainland ruling and built their houses with swallowtail roofs. The Grand Hotel in Taipei is believed to have the biggest classical swallowtail roof in the world. Ordinary people could build only horseback roofs that were rounded and shaped like a horse's back; these became characteristic of traditional farmhouses in Taiwan.

Modern architecture since the 1970s has increasingly been influenced by international architectural styles, and most apartment buildings in Taipei are very similar in style to those in Western countries. However, one important aspect of Chinese architecture that still has an impact

The Chiang Kai-shek Memorial Park in Taipei. The swallowtail roof style is seen here.

on Taiwan's buildings is feng shui (FUHNG shway), or geomancy. Literally "wind and water," this is an Eastern practice based on the belief that nonliving objects can influence people's living environment. In accordance with feng shui, building construction in Taiwan follows certain fundamental principles. An important principle is that the front and back doors should not face each other directly in a straight line as this would allow good luck to pass right through and out of a building without stopping for a visit.

ART TREASURES OF CHINA

Taiwan's most prized collection of art treasures is housed in the famous National Palace Museum in Taipei. There are over 620,000 artifacts in this fabulous collection, which is believed to be priceless. Many artifacts in the museum are from the Chinese imperial collection that began in the Sung dynasty over 1,000 years ago. These were taken to Taiwan by the KMT, led by Chiang Kai-shek, when the party fled the Communist revolution on the mainland in 1949. During the Cultural Revolution in Communist China, many historical and art treasures were systematically destroyed as a result of government policy. Taiwan's collection of Chinese historical and art treasures is now believed to be the most extensive in the world.

LEISURE

THE TAIWANESE ARE A SOCIABLE people who like spending time with family and friends. On weekends people take time off from their busy schedules to enjoy themselves. On Saturday nights they go out for dinner with their families or meet friends. Ever since the Taiwanese began to receive higher wages in the 1980s, they have spent more on recreation. Taiwanese tend to use their leisure time mainly by engaging in sporting activities. Going to the movies or the theater are also favorite pastimes.

OUTINGS IN THE PARK

The park is a very important venue for leisure activities in Taiwan. Almost every day city parks are thronged with people walking, exercising, meditating, gossiping, or just relaxing. Weekends are even busier as whole families turn up to enjoy the fresh air and scenery.

Early morning is the best time to exercise in the park. This is when hundreds of people, young and old, head to the park to exercise before going to school or work. Among the different ways of working out are tai chi, dancing, calisthenics, and racket games, such as badminton. Among the older generation, it is common to see men playing Chinese chess in the park. Some even bring portable music players and hold singing sessions there.

OTHER ACTIVITIES

Besides spending time in the parks, many families eat out on Saturdays and Sundays or go shopping. Taipei's shopping malls are crowded with

Above: **A family visiting Window on China, a park that is about an hour's drive from Taipei. It has miniature replicas of many famous landmarks in Taiwan and mainland China.**

Opposite: **Two Taiwanese men play Chinese chess while another looks on in interest.**

Engrossed Taiwanese teenagers play computer games at a computer game trade show in Taipei.

people, and night markets bustle with shoppers. Shihlin Night Market is one of the largest night markets in Taipei, and the flower and jade markets also attract shoppers. Taipei's exotic Snake Alley bustles with buyers and the curious—the marketplace sells everything from snakes to medicinal potions made from animal extracts.

Some families visit temples on Sundays, and other families visit the National Palace Museum, the zoo, or one of the many new amusement parks. Playing mahjong (MAH-johng) is popular with adults, and *pachinko* (PAH-chin-koh), a Japanese word for pinball machines, is another way for adults and children to pass the time. Taiwanese teenagers go to the movies, meet their friends in parks, or hold barbeques. When it rains or is too cold, young people get together in amusement arcades to bowl or to play pool, table tennis, and computer games.

CHINESE-STYLE WORKOUTS

Some forms of exercise that are unique to the Chinese are based on the martial arts. Tai chi chuan (TAI jee CHWAHN), or tai chi for short, is the ancient Chinese art of shadowboxing. It is actually a form of exercise with a series of set meditative movements, sometimes performed to music. The graceful movements exercise the muscles, enhance breathing, and are believed to stimulate the digestive and nervous systems. Chinese-style kung fu (KOONG foo) is also a popular martial art and forms part of the physical education curriculum in schools.

The ideal time to practice tai chi or any other martial art is in the early morning, when chi, the life force or energy believed to be embodied in every living thing, is at its peak. Martial art displays can be seen daily in Taipei's city parks, at Sun Yat-sen Memorial Hall, and at Yang-ming -shan National Park.

GETTING AWAY

Taiwan's dramatic mountain scenery offers city dwellers the opportunity to get away from the noise and stress of city life. Hiking in the Central Mountain Range has become a popular leisure pastime, and hiking clubs in Taiwan enjoy a growing popularity. Evergreen forests cover two-thirds of the island, and hikers can enjoy scenic views of forests, plains, waterfalls, and lakes.

Yü Shan National Park is a favorite destination of many. The largest and most pristine national park in Taiwan, Yü Shan offers hiking trails and showcases the ruins of aboriginal settlements and the Qing dynasty. Another popular locale for enthusiastic hikers is Hsueh Shan, the second highest mountain in Taiwan. Standing at an impressive height of 10,321 feet (3,146 m), Hohuan Shan (meaning Mountain of Harmonious

In Chinese kung fu a distinction is made between external and internal kung fu. It is said that in external kung fu the muscles, bones, and skin are exercised. In internal kung fu the spirit, mind, and internal life force are trained. The higher one's level of achievement in kung fu, the better one's ability to maintain good health and to live a long, active life.

The unique landscape of Yehliu makes it a favorite destination. The sandstone rocky layer is subject to erosion and earth movements, which caused the strange formations.

Joy) in the Central Mountain Range is Taiwan's only ski resort. Besides drawing skiers in winter, it attracts numerous hikers during summer.

The Taiwanese also enjoy traveling to mountain resorts to take in the scenery. The tranquil beauty of Sun Moon Lake makes it a favorite destination among honeymooners and tourists. Ali Shan, with views of 18 mountain peaks in the Central Mountain Range and the grand Taroko Gorge, also boasts a popular resort. A favorite excursion from Taipei involves a trip to the shore. The dramatic, rocky, coastal scenery of Yehliu in the northern part of the island draws many of Taipei's residents who like to visit the area on weekends.

SPORTS

The most popular sports in Taiwan are basketball, baseball, and table tennis. These games are played by children in schools and have a wide

110

following among adults as well. Many Taiwanese are also learning to play golf and tennis. Baseball is played widely by both boys and girls in elementary and junior high schools. Taiwan has over 220 amateur teams and more than 1,000 Little Leagues. In 2001 Taiwan hosted the baseball World Cup and took a respectable third place. Baseball games are aired on television, and the Chinese Professional Baseball League season that lasts from March to October is closely followed by fans every year.

Basketball, introduced to Taiwan by Nationalist soldiers, attracted a large following until 1989, when Taipei's Chunghua Stadium burned down. It is enjoying a resurgence, and there are now two professional leagues.

TRADITIONAL SPORTS

Skipping with a jump rope has been popular since the Tang dynasty and is promoted in calisthenics exercises in schools. Shuttlecock is described in historical records of the Han and Sung dynasties. The object is to kick a shuttlecock back and forth and keep it from falling to the ground. Top spinning became popular during the Sung dynasty. Although the game was once popular with children, it is played mainly by men in Taiwan today. Diabolo spinning is taught in schools. The diabolo looks like a large yo-yo; it has two wooden or plastic wheels with a shaft between them. The player moves the diabolo by using a long cotton string attached to a stick at either end of the string.

KTV ENTERTAINMENT

Karaoke Television (KTV), or singing along to prerecorded music videos, is a popular activity for socializing in Taiwan. Karaoke is actually a Japanese word meaning "empty orchestra." Karaoke clubs offer private rooms with television sets, music videos, and a microphone.

Taiwan places great importance on promoting sports in schools— athletic aptitude classes have been set up in elementary and high schools, and young athletes are groomed to take part in international games, such as the Asian Games and the Olympics.

FESTIVALS

THE CALENDAR OF FESTIVALS in Taiwan kicks off every year with the Lunar New Year. This is a tradition that dates back to a time when Chinese society was based on agriculture. Because people were dependent on the weather for their livelihood, festivals marked the passing of the seasons. For instance, the Lunar New Year falls in winter, when farmers cannot work in the fields, leaving them free time to celebrate. Tomb-Sweeping Day falls between the spring plowing and summer weeding, and the Mid-Autumn Festival is held around the final harvest of the year, when people can begin to relax. At festival celebrations different generations within a family reaffirm their bonds. They are occasions for rest and relaxation when people take time off from work and their busy lifestyles.

Left: **A tug-of-war during an aboriginal festival. Aboriginal celebrations are based on ancient beliefs; rituals involving song and dance are a fundamental component of these colorful festivals. These gatherings are also occasions for competitions and social interaction, where young unmarried people meet and find prospective marriage partners.**

Opposite: **Taiwanese people release "sky lanterns" to celebrate the traditional Chinese Lantern Festival on the first full moon of the Lunar New Year. The lanterns are released in the belief that they will bestow good luck and blessings.**

FESTIVALS AND NATIONAL HOLIDAYS

Foundation of the Republic of China Day	January 1
Lunar New Year	January 29 (varies)
Women's Day	March 8
Youth Day	March 29
Children's Day	April 4
Tomb-Sweeping Day	April 5
Labor Day	May 1
Dragon Boat Festival	5th day of 5th lunar month
Ghost Festival	7th lunar month
Confucius's Birthday	September 28
Mid-Autumn Festival	15th day of 8th lunar month
Double Ten or National Day	October 10
Retrocession Day	October 25
Chiang Kai-shek's Birthday	October 31
Sun Yat-sen's Birthday	November 12

Double Ten is the most colorful of all the secular holidays. This is the occasion for huge rallies, parades with lion and dragon dances, and displays of martial arts, acrobatics, and folk dances. The grand finale is a splendid fireworks display.

MAJOR NATIONAL HOLIDAYS

The Foundation of the Republic of China Day on January 1 is the anniversary of the date when Sun Yat-sen was sworn in as the first president of the Republic of China. Double Ten Day, or National Day, on October 10 marks the fall of the Qing dynasty and the establishment of the Republic of China. Retrocession Day on October 25 is the anniversary of the day in 1945 when the Japanese occupation of Taiwan ended and the island returned to Chinese rule. The birthdays of two important historic figures in the Republic of China's history are also celebrated: Sun Yat-sen's birthday on November 12, and Chiang Kai-shek's birthday on October 31. Constitution Day on December 25 commemorates the day in 1947 when the constitution of the Republic of China on Taiwan came into force.

LUNAR NEW YEAR

The Lunar New Year, or Chinese New Year, is the single most important festival of every Chinese community anywhere in the world. It usually

falls in late January or early February, depending on variations in the lunar calendar. The festival actually lasts for 15 days, but only New Year's Eve and the first two days are public holidays in Taiwan. However, most offices and shops close during the first week of the Lunar New Year.

The weeks leading up to the new year are a busy time for most people. To make sure they get off to a good start in the year ahead, people stock up on food, buy new clothes, spring-clean, and decorate their houses with Chinese characters inviting good luck.

One of the highlights of this festival is the traditional family reunion dinner. On the eve of the Lunar New Year, family members, who may be living far away, return to their parents' home to share in a lavish dinner. The children have a great time. They are given "lucky money" in red envelopes, or *hung bao*. Families relax after dinner, catch up on the local gossip, and stay up through the night to welcome the New Year. Finally fireworks are set off to frighten away evil spirits.

On the eve of the Lunar New Year in Taiwan, it is traditional for children to kneel and wish their elders good luck and longevity. In return, they are given red envelopes containing money as a form of blessing.

Lion *(above)* **and dragon dances are performed on various auspicious occasions, including the Lunar New Year.**

The second day of the Lunar New Year is when family members remember their ancestors and offer sacrifices. Ritual offerings are made to ancestors at the family shrine, followed by offerings to the gods at temples, with prayers asking for a happy and prosperous year. Family members also visit each other with the traditional greeting of *kung hsi fa tsai* (KOHNG see fah TSAI). People stay at home on the third day because this is when bad luck is believed to be in the air. The next few days are a time of increased activity: firecrackers are set off to welcome the gods, offerings are made to them, and sacrificial money is burned.

The sixth day is the birthday of the god Tsu Shih, and the seventh day is believed to be the anniversary of the creation of human beings. The ninth day is another day for making offerings as it is the birthday of the Jade Emperor, the supreme deity of the Taoist religion.

The Lantern Festival on the 15th day traditionally marks the end of the Lunar New Year festival. This is an especially happy time for children, who play a major role in this part of the festival. The ancient Chinese believed that celestial spirits could be seen in the first full moon of the lunar year, and people lit lanterns to see the spirits. Today, children carry on this tradition in temples, parks, and streets all over Taiwan.

Sticky-rice dumplings called *yuan hsiao* (YOO-ahn SEE-ow) are eaten at this time. The dumplings are round to symbolize the full moon and the unity of the family. In Taiwanese society, where age is looked upon with great respect, there is a common saying that people will not gain a year in age until they eat a *yuan hsiao*.

Tomb-Sweeping Day has its roots in the deep attachment the Chinese feel for the land from which they originated and for their ancestors. Their long history as an agricultural society has bred a profound reverence for the land that has nurtured so many generations.

TOMB-SWEEPING DAY

Tomb-Sweeping Day is observed on April 5, which is also the anniversary of the death of President Chiang Kai-shek. This day is an important ancestral festival when the Taiwanese remember their deceased family members. Entire families visit the graves of their ancestors and offer prayers to them. The graves are swept free of dirt, and fresh flowers and offerings of food and wine are placed in front of the tombs. The ceremony must be performed before dawn or in the early morning because it is necessary that the spirits of the departed, who sleep during the night, still be "at home" in their tombs.

A poem from the Tang dynasty describes the intense emotional bond living people feel for their departed ancestors:

On Tomb-Sweeping Day as the rain falls everywhere, people walking in the streets feel the sorrow within and without.

The Taiwanese believe they fulfill their obligation of filial respect and please their ancestors by remembering them on Tomb-Sweeping Day.

Taiwanese men participate in a Dragon Boat Festival race on the Chi-lung River in Taipei. The annual race is held on the fifth day of the fifth Chinese lunar month.

DRAGON BOAT FESTIVAL

The Dragon Boat Festival commemorates the death of Chu Yuan, a scholar-statesman of the Warring States period (475–221 B.C.) during the Zhou dynasty, who drowned himself in a river in protest against tyranny and corruption. The legend is that upon his death, those who respected his honesty and sacrifice went out in boats to search for his body. When they could not find it, they threw cooked rice into the river so that the fish would not eat Chu Yuan's body. On the fifth day of the fifth lunar month, teams take part in dragon boat races to commemorate the search for Chu Yuan. The most famous race today is the one in Taipei, where teams from all over the country vie for the Chiang Kai-shek Memorial Cup. Dragon boats today are about 43 feet (13 m) long and have a helmsman, a drummer, 22 oarsmen, and a flag catcher. Women's dragon boat races use smaller boats.

Another custom is the eating of *tzung tzu* (JONG tze), a rice dumpling stuffed with pork or beans. This is in memory of the people who threw rice into the river to keep the fish from eating Chu Yuan's body.

GHOST MONTH

The Chinese believe that the ghosts of the dead return to earth for a visit during the seventh lunar month. To appease these spirits and prevent them from causing harm, the Taiwanese offer them prayers, food, wine, and sacrificial paper money. Both Buddhist and Taoist priests perform prayer rites in their temples every day during this month. Lanterns are hung on bamboo poles in temple courtyards to invite the ghosts to enter and listen to the prayers offered to them. It is regarded as inauspicious to conduct weddings and new business ventures during this month.

MID-AUTUMN FESTIVAL

This festival celebrates the appearance of the biggest and brightest full moon of the year, which coincides with the end of the harvest. The Taiwanese make a family event of this festival. Typically, all members of the family will go to parks to gaze at "the Lady in the Moon" and to eat mooncakes.

It is believed that the Lady in the Moon was once the wife of a Tang emperor. She drank a magic potion and flew up to the moon, where she has been ever since.

Mooncakes are round pastries stuffed with sweet bean paste. They have a historical symbolism for the Chinese, being a reminder of the time during the Yuan dynasty when China was ruled by the Mongols. To overthrow the Mongols, people had to rally enough support to start a rebellion, and messages hidden in mooncakes were passed around for this purpose.

To the Chinese, ghosts are merely living beings who have passed on into a spiritual form of existence. They must eat and drink. The descendants of these spirits take care of them by making offerings of food, wine, and "ghost" money.

Members of the Ami aboriginal people in traditional red and black dress celebrate the Harvest Festival.

ABORIGINAL FESTIVALS

Aboriginal festivals are colorful occasions celebrated with a great sense of ceremony and pageantry. Many aborigines who have moved to the cities and assimilated with the Chinese make a point of returning to their home villages to celebrate various festivals.

HARVEST FESTIVAL The Harvest Festival celebrated by the Ami is one of the most important aboriginal festivals. It lasts for seven days in late summer, at the end of the harvest season. During the first three days of the festival people sit down to talk about what they have achieved in the past year. This is followed by singing and dancing in the village square.

During this time the Ami also have a Proposal Festival for the unmarried. Young people spend time together to get acquainted, and on the last night of the Harvest Festival, a young woman chooses the man she wants to get engaged to by obtaining his belt. A chosen man then sends 20 bundles of firewood to the woman's family; if these are accepted, the engagement becomes official.

FLYING FISH FESTIVAL This festival, which is observed by the Yami, is based on an ancient myth about a talking fish that taught the tribe to follow a strict set of rules concerning the catching and eating of fish. According to legend, two Yami fishermen caught a huge winged fish that could fly. A little later, the fishermen's families found sores breaking out on their skin. The tribal elder then had a dream about a fish called Blackfin, who asked to meet him the next day. Blackfin actually appeared before the old man the next day and taught him the rituals and ceremonies associated with the fishing season and the catching of flying fish.

To this day, the Yami still observe these rituals. At the start of the flying fish season, all Yami men put on ceremonial dress with silver caps and beautiful jewelry and go out to sea in decorated boats to catch flying fish. These fish are considered to be special and are not cooked in the same pots as other fish.

FESTIVAL OF THE LITTLE PEOPLE The origin of this Saisiyat festival is told in a story dating back 500 years. At the time, the Saisiyat were not good farmers, but they managed to learn farming techniques from a group of pygmies. Unfortunately, the two peoples quarreled, and the Saisiyat killed the pygmies. After that, the Saisiyat became afraid that the spirits of the pygmies would take revenge, so they held a festival to appease and exorcise the spirits.

The theme of this festival still lies in appeasing the pygmy spirits through song and dance. The spirits are invited to attend the festival with ritual singing and dancing that lasts the whole night. Over the next few days the pygmy spirits are greeted and entertained with more traditional songs and dances. On the seventh and last day, a small tree is placed over the spirit shrine. Young Saisiyat men then proceed to exorcise the spirits by throwing pieces of the tree at the eastern sky and by staging an aggressive dance to frighten away the spirits.

Legends play an important part in aboriginal festivals. In the Yami festival of the flying fish, for example, the rituals are decided by the commandments of a legendary fish. To this day, the Yami destroy old fish-drying racks and build new ones, and put new fences around each house, before the annual festival; on the day itself, they allow no strangers to visit.

FOOD

CHINESE CUISINE IS WIDELY acknowledged to be one of the most refined and sophisticated in the world. This is not surprising considering that food preparation has been an important part of Chinese history and culture for over 2,000 years. In fact, in the fourth century A.D., a cookbook called *Shih-Chin* (SHUH-chin) was published in China—probably one of the first cookbooks ever produced in the history of the world!

Although the lifestyle of the Taiwanese has been affected by modernization and Western influences, in the culinary field Chinese food reigns supreme. The Taiwanese still prefer to eat traditional Chinese dishes instead of Western food. An exception to this is the Taiwanese fondness for hamburgers—it is considered very fashionable to eat at popular hamburger restaurants.

As in other parts of Asia, rice or *fan* (fahn) is the most important staple, especially for the Taiwanese who migrated from southern China. In just about every meal, dishes of meat and vegetables are eaten with rice. Many food products are also made from rice. There are rice cakes, rice noodles, rice congee (porridge), and rice wine. In fact, eating and rice are such a central part of the Chinese culture that many conversations begin with the heartwarming greeting, *"Chi fan le mei you?"* (CHUH fahn luh may yoh), meaning "Have you eaten rice?" or "Have you had your meal?" Chinese cooking is also famous for its noodles, although noodles are mainly a feature of northern Chinese food.

Above: **Freshly made noodles are sold daily at grocery stalls and are popular with the Taiwanese people.**

Opposite: **A food vendor at one of Taiwan's numerous night markets sells a variety of popular Taiwanese snacks.**

The Taiwanese take pains to present their food in a colorful and appetizing manner, and carved vegetables are often used as a decorative garnish.

COOKING STYLES

As immigrants from the mainland settled in Taiwan over the centuries, they took with them cuisines from different parts of mainland China. In a country as vast as China, many regions have evolved their own styles of cooking, and these styles are named after the regions in which they first originated.

The Szechuan style, with its hot and spicy dishes originating from Szechuan Province, is one of the most popular cooking styles in Taiwan. A famous Szechuan dish is camphor- and tea-smoked duck. The duck is marinated in a flavoring of ginger, cinnamon, peppercorns, orange peel, and coriander, and then steamed. What gives this dish its distinctive flavor and name is the next stage, when the duck is smoked over a charcoal fire made aromatic with tea leaves and camphor wood.

Hunanese food from Hunan Province is hot and spicy or sweet and sour. Honey ham and frogs' legs in chili sauce are specialties of this province. Beggar's chicken, a well-known dish in Taiwan, is also of Hunanese origin. According to legend, there was once a poor man who stole a chicken. When he saw some guards approaching, he covered the chicken with mud and threw it into a fire. After the guards had left, the man cracked open the dried mud and found a fragrant cooked chicken.

Hakka food, also from Hunan province, is simple, country-style fare. There are no fancy sauces, and the dishes are mostly pork-based.

Szechuan and Hunanese food represent the western Chinese style of cooking. Northern cuisine is seen in the Peking and Mongolian cooking styles. Peking cuisine features more wheat-based food and less rice. Lamb is a part of its menu. Mongolian barbecues, where meat and vegetables are grilled on a large hot plate, are very popular in Taiwan.

Cantonese food from southern China is bland in comparison with other styles as it has minimal flavoring. Most dishes are stir-fried or steamed. Cantonese food is perhaps the best known Chinese food in the West because most Chinese immigrants to Europe and America were Cantonese and cooked in the Cantonese style when they set up restaurants.

The eastern style of cooking is seen in Shanghainese food, another popular cuisine in Taiwan. This usually features rich and slightly sweet sauces and is well known for its range of seafood dishes. Taiwanese food is indigenous to Taiwan. It is similar to Shanghainese food in that it features a lot of seafood and uses the same seasonings. It also uses lots of seafood, as well as taro, radishes, and sweet potatoes—all of which grow well in Taiwan. Popular dishes are salted radish omelet and three-cups chicken (which can also be made with frog). Three-cups dishes are

Taiwanese food uses a wide range of seafood, including fish, shrimp, crab, eel, squid, scallop, shellfish, shark's fin, and sea cucumber.

125

made with soy sauce, rice wine, and sesame oil—all measured out in cups. Recipes today, however, use less oil. In night markets, many Taiwanese enjoy another traditional Taiwanese snack—the oyster omelet.

MEALS AND MEALTIMES

Traditional Chinese breakfasts usually include bread, eggs, and milk—but with a difference. The bread is not Western-style bread but rather consists of traditional steamed rolls or deep-fried dough sticks called *you tiao* (YOO ti-ow), and milk is not dairy milk but

Food stalls are a popular alternative to eating out in a restaurant. They offer a good variety of food and are cheap in comparison.

soybean milk. Fried eggs usually accompany these. Another breakfast dish is congee, a rice porridge with a savory fish, chicken, or pork flavoring. The Taiwanese place great importance on having at least a light meal each morning, so it is not common to skip breakfast. However, breakfast tends to be a quick meal for family members who have to rush off to work or school.

For most working people, lunch is also a quick meal. Some people pack a lunch box of rice with some meat and vegetables, but many others eat at outdoor food stalls or restaurants that cater to the lunchtime crowd.

MUNCH ATTACK!

Whenever the Taiwanese feel like munching on something, they are likely to reach for *kua chi* (GUAH tze). The shell of the *kua chi,* or dried watermelon seed, is cracked open with the teeth, and the nut inside is eaten as a snack.

THE CULTURE OF TEA—*CHA* AND *YUM CHA*

Tea drinking is an important cultural and gastronomic institution in Taiwan. It is polite and sociable to invite someone to have tea, so every visitor is automatically offered a cup of *cha* (chah), or tea.

Tea is made from tea leaves that are treated in different ways. Green tea is made from unfermented leaves; black tea is fully fermented and has an aroma of malt; and oolong tea, or "black dragon tea," is partially fermented. Other teas are made from blends of tea leaves and flowers, such as jasmine and chrysanthemum. Tea is one of Taiwan's agricultural products that grows best in a subtropical climate at a high elevation.

Chinese tea is made by pouring boiling water onto tea leaves and leaving this to steep for a few minutes. No milk or sugar is added, so all one tastes is the flavor of the

tea. A certain ritual is attached to brewing tea. First, a small teapot, ideally made of copper-colored pottery, is warmed by pouring boiling water into it. This water is then discarded. Fresh boiling water is again poured into the teapot and tea leaves added, but the first brew of the tea is not drunk. It is poured away instead. Tea and boiling water are then placed into the teapot a second time and left to steep for a minute or two. It is only then that the tea is poured into little cups to be drunk. The flaky tea leaves are not strained but left to float on top. Since the leaves are bitter, people avoid swallowing them by holding up the cup and blowing gently on the tea. This pushes the leaves away so that they can sip the tea without taking in the leaves.

Tea drinking is an important national institution. This is reflected in the number of tea houses where people meet to drink tea, munch on snacks, read, relax, and even conduct business. The culture of tea drinking is so strong that it has spawned a variety of savory snacks to go with it. The snacks are called *yum cha* (YAHM chah) in Taiwan. They are actually a Cantonese invention known in the West as dim sum (DIM sum, a Cantonese term) and in China as *tien hsin* (DEE-yen sin). Tea snacks are believed to have originated 600 years ago during the Yuan dynasty.

Several members of a family enjoying a meal together. Family dinners often feature many different dishes and can last a long time.

In most homes the Taiwanese tend to have dinner between 6:00 and 7:00 P.M. when family members return from work. Dinner usually consists of a hot soup, rice or noodles, and two or three other dishes of meat or seafood and vegetables. Desserts are not featured widely in Chinese meals, particularly at home, but fruit is normally eaten after dinner, as the Taiwanese believe this helps digestion and clears the palate.

EATING OUT

The eating habits of Taiwanese people have been affected, to some degree, by modern urban living. Hence, while it used to be the case that most Taiwanese would eat at home most of the time, many urban-dwelling, working Taiwanese eat out quite a lot nowadays and often in informal, family-style stalls and eateries. Whether at home or in a restaurant, the Taiwanese observe traditional etiquette associated with eating. For example, meals must be eaten while seated, and there is a particular order to who may be seated first among the men and women, young and old. Meals are served at round tables, and each table can usually seat up to 10 or 12 persons.

At restaurants the host usually places the orders, but it is considered polite for the host to ask guests to suggest dishes. The meal usually starts with a cold dish of appetizers. Dishes are brought in course after course. They are placed in the center of the table on a rotating turntable and everyone helps themselves to a little of each dish. Dining etiquette demands that one selects pieces of food closest to one and not stretch for a choice bit. The main courses are eaten with chopsticks, and soup is sipped from a spoon. The last dish is usually a plate of fried rice or noodles.

At dinner parties, toasts are often exchanged. There is a particular ritual and etiquette to making toasts—it is considered polite to hold the glass with one hand and to have the other hand touching the base of the glass. The host usually makes a toast at the beginning of the meal by saying "*kan pei*" (GAHN bay), meaning "bottoms up." If the person making the toast says *suei yi* (SWAY yi), meaning "as you please," the others present may either take a sip of their drink or drink up completely—as they please.

YIN AND YANG FOOD

The Chinese believe that all types of food can be categorized into three basic types. Hot, or yang (yahng), food heats the blood and reduces vital energy, whereas cold, or yin, food cools the blood and increases vital energy. Neutral, or *ping*, foods are balanced and do not affect energy either way.

Yang foods are usually favored in winter, when the blood needs to be warmed, and cooling yin foods beat the heat of summer. When ordering meals in restaurants, the Taiwanese aim to achieve a balance of all three types of food—fried foods are yang and are balanced with steamed, or yin, foods; meat dishes (yang) are balanced with vegetables (yin); and yang spices are balanced with yin fruits.

The Chinese have long held a traditional belief in the medicinal value of food. Many plants used in Chinese cooking, such as scallions, ginger, garlic, dried lily buds, and tree fungus, are believed to have properties of preventing or alleviating various illnesses.

SAN BEI JI (TAIWAN STYLE CHICKEN WITH 3-CUP SAUCE)

This recipe makes 4 servings.

10^1/$_2$ ounces (300 gram) chicken breasts, skinned and deboned
3–4 tablespoons sesame or peanut oil
10 thin slices ginger
2 or 3 cloves of garlic, chopped
1 stalk green onion (scallion), chopped
Approximately 3–4 tablespoons minced red pepper
1 cup (237 ml) light soy sauce
1 cup (237 ml) rice wine
2 tablespoons sugar

Wash the chicken and cut it into bite-size pieces. Heat a wok or large frying pan, pour in the sesame oil and let it heat at high temperature until it boils. Add the ginger, garlic, onion, and red pepper while the oil boils. Next, carefully add the chicken meat to the hot oil and stir-fry the ingredients well. Add the soy sauce, and continue to stir. Pour in the rice wine and sugar, stir well, and cover the wok. Cook the meat at medium heat for approximately five minutes until the gravy has almost dried up. Sprinkle the meat with the onion and serve with cooked rice. This dish can also be cooked in a medium-sized clay cooking pot to retain the flavor of the meat better.

COCONUT PUDDING

This recipe makes 4 servings.

$^1/_2$ ounce (14 gram) unflavored gelatin
$1^5/_8$ cups (384 ml) boiling water
5 ounces (142 gram) evaporated milk
7 ounces (198 gram) white sugar
1 teaspoon (5 ml) coconut extract
2 egg whites

Into a heat-resistant, large bowl, pour the boiling water and dissolve the gelatin in it. Stir in the evaporated milk, sugar, and coconut extract. Allow the hot mixture to cool to room temperature. When the gelatin mixture has cooled to room temperature, place the bowl in an ice bath. Whip the egg whites until they are fluffy. When the mixture begins to set, fold the egg whites into it. Lightly grease a baking mold. Spread the mixture into the mold and refrigerate it for twenty minutes or until it sets.

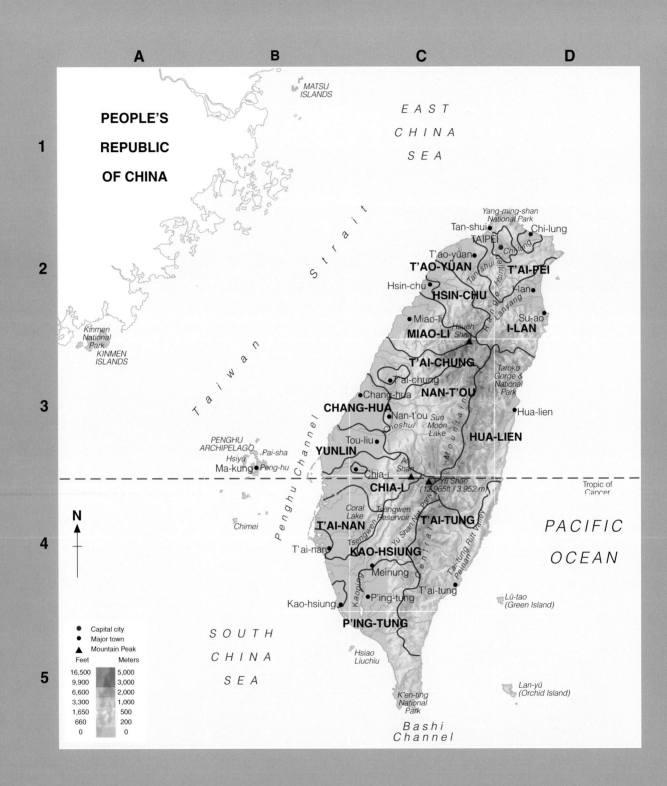

PEOPLE'S

REPUBLIC

OF CHINA

MATSU ISLANDS

E A S T

C H I N A

S E A

Yang-ming-shan
National Park

Tan-shui ● ● Chi-lung
● TAIPEI
T'ao-yüan ●
T'AO-YÜAN ● Chi-lung **T'AI-PEI**

Hsin-chu ●
HSIN-CHU ● I-lan

● Miao-li Su-ao ●
MIAO-LI Hsüeh **I-LAN**
Shan ▲

*Kinmen
National
Park*

*KINMEN
ISLANDS*

T'AI-CHUNG
T'ai-chung ●
*Taroko
Gorge &
National
Park*
● Chang-hua **NAN-T'OU**
CHANG-HUA
Nan-t'ou ● *Sun
Choshui Moon
Lake*
● Hua-lien
HUA-LIEN

*T
a
i
w
a
n*

*S
t
r
a
i
t*

Tou-liu ●
YUNLIN

*PENGHU
ARCHIPELAGO*

Hsiyü *Pai-sha*
Ma-kung ● ● Peng-hu

*P
e
n
g
h
u

C
h
a
n
n
e
l*

Ai
Chia-i ● Shan
▲ ▲ Yu Shan
CHIA-I (12,965ft / 3,952 m)

*Tropic of
Cancer*

Chimei

*Coral
Lake*
*Tsengwen
Reservoir*
T'AI-NAN
Tsengwen
T'ai-nan ●
KAO-HSIUNG

T'AI-TUNG

*PACIFIC
OCEAN*

Ta-tung Rift Valley
Peinan

● Meinung
Kaoping
Kao-hsiung ● ● P'ing-tung
P'ING-TUNG

● T'ai-tung

*Lü-tao
(Green Island)*

N

S O U T H

C H I N A

S E A

*Hsiao
Liuchiu*

*K'en-ting
National
Park*

*Lan-yü
(Orchid Island)*

*B a s h i
C h a n n e l*

● Capital city
● Major town
▲ Mountain Peak

Feet	Meters
16,500	5,000
9,900	3,000
6,600	2,000
3,300	1,000
1,650	500
660	200
0	0

MAP OF TAIWAN

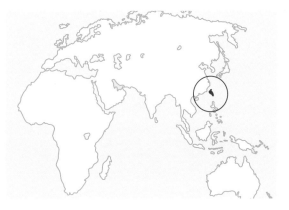

ECONOMIC TAIWAN

Services

- Airport
- Nuclear power plant
- Port
- Railway

Agriculture

- Flowers
- Fruits
- Pig rearing
- Poultry
- Rice
- Tea
- Vegetables

Natural Resources

- Fish

Industry

- Aviation & aerospac
- Biotechnology
- Cement
- Chemicals
- Consumer products
- Electronics
- Iron & steel
- Petroleum refining
- Pharmaceuticals

ABOUT THE ECONOMY

GROSS DOMESTIC PRODUCT (GDP)
$610.8 billion (2005 estimate)

GDP PER CAPITA
US$26,700 (2005 estimate)

GDP BY SECTOR
(Percentage of total GDP)
Manufacturing 25.5 percent; finance, insurance, and real estate 21.5 percent; commerce, 19.1 percent; government service 10.9 percent; transport and communications 7.1 percent; agriculture, forestry, and fishing 1.7 percent
(2004 estimates)

LAND USE
Arable land 24 percent, permanent crops 1 percent, other uses 75 percent (2001 estimate)

AGRICULTURAL PRODUCTS
Rice, betel nuts, bamboo shoots, sugarcane, peanuts, mangoes, watermelons, tea, corn

INDUSTRIAL PRODUCTS
Information technology, electronics, electrical equipment, textiles, chemicals, petrochemicals

CURRENCY
New Taiwan Dollar (NT$) = 100 cents
Notes denominations: NT$1000, 500, 200, 100, 50
Coin denominations: NT$50, 10, 5, 1
USD 1 = NT$31.71 (2005)

INFLATION RATE
1.8 percent (2005 estimate)

MAJOR TRADE PARTNERS
Japan, China, Hong Kong, United States, South Korea (2004 estimate)

TOTAL EXPORTS
$170.5 billion (2004 estimate)

TOTAL IMPORTS
$165 billion (2004 estimate)

LABOR FORCE
10.31 million (2005 estimate)

WORKFORCE BY SECTOR
Agriculture 6 percent; industry 35.8 percent; services 58.2 percent (2005 estimates)

UNEMPLOYMENT RATE
4.2 percent (2005 estimate)

PORTS AND HARBORS
Chi-lung, Kao-hsiung, Su-ao, T'ai-chung

AIRPORTS
40; 38 with paved runways (2005 estimate)

COMMUNICATIONS MEDIA
Telephone: 13.4 million operating main lines (2003 estimate)
Mobile cell phone: 25.1 million (2003 estimate)
Television: 400 sets per 1,000 persons (2000 estimate)
Internet: 2.8 million hosts (2003 estimate), 13.8 million users (2005 estimate).

CULTURAL TAIWAN

Formosan Aboriginal Culture Village
The Formosan Aboriginal Culture Village is a showcase of the culture and traditions of Taiwan's indigenous peoples.

Sun Moon Lake
Located at the geographical center of Taiwan, the lake is a picturesque tourist attraction containing emerald waters and surrounded by mountains. The Formosan Aboriginal Culture Village is nearby.

Chia i
The city functions mainly as a departure point from which excursions to the Central Mountain Range can be made. Industrial activity is less concentrated here than in other cities, with most parts of the city centered on manufacturing.

Matsu Temple at Deer Ear Gate
Almost 400 years old, this temple is dedicated to the Goddess of the Sea and is also home to the Old Man under the Moon, a Taoist god somewhat like Cupid. Singles who are looking for a spouse pray to this god.

Lungshan Temple
One of Taiwan's oldest and most famous temples, it is a striking showcase of temple architecture.

Taipei
The political, cultural, and economic center of Taiwan, Taipei is the largest city of the land.

T'ai-nan
The former capital of Taiwan is also its oldest city. T'ai-nan is best known as the cultural and historic center of the island.

Yang-ming-shan National Park
In this park, visitors can experience the vast variety of nature's creations, such as waterfalls, volcanic craters, lakes, and hot springs.

Chiang Kai-shek Memorial Hall
Taiwan's monument to its late president greets visitors with a Ming-style arch at its main entrance. The Hall is flanked by the National Theater and the National Concert Hall.

National Palace Museum
Here, at the National Palace Museum, exhibits of Chinese culture from as far back as the Northern Sung dynasty to the more recent Qing dynasty can be viewed. The museum has one of the most comprehensive collections of Chinese art in the world with more than 700,000 items on display.

Yü Shan (Jade Mountain)
This is the highest mountain in the Central Ranges.

The Cave of Eight Immortals
Also known as *Pahsien Tung* (PAH-Hsien Tung) in Chinese, there are actually 14 caves located in this area. It has been designated as a site of national archaeological importance due to the discovery of numerous artifacts.

ABOUT THE CULTURE

OFFICIAL NAME
Republic of China
(Pronounced as JONG-hua MIN-GUO in Chinese)

CAPITAL
Taipei

NATIONAL FLAG
Known as "a white sun in blue sky" and first made official on October 8, 1928, the 12 points or rays of the white sun in the republic's national flag represent 12 two-hour periods of the 24-hour day and symbolize unceasing progress. The blue, white, and red colors represent the Three Principles of the People set out by Sun Yat-sen.

NATIONAL ANTHEM
Often called "San Min Chu I" (SAN Min JOO Ee), meaning the Three Principles of the People, which is taken from the first line of the anthem. The "San Min Chu I" is not allowed to be performed on mainland China.

NATIONAL FLOWER
Prunus mei (plum blossom)

HIGHEST POINT
Yü Shan (12,965 feet or 3,952 m)

MAJOR RIVERS
Kaoping, Choshui, Tan-shui

MAJOR LAKES
Tsengwen Reservoir, Coral Lake, Sun Moon Lake

MAJOR CITIES
Taipei, Kao-hsiung, T'ai-chung, T'ai-nan

ADMINISTRATIVE DIVISIONS
Counties: Chang-hua, Chia-i, Hsin-chu, Hua-lien, I-lan, Kao-hsiung, Kinmen, Lien-chiang, Miao-li, Nan-t'ou, Peng-hu, Ping-tung, T'ai-chung, T'ai-nan, T'ai-pei, T'ai-tung, T'ao-yüan, Yun-lin
Municipalities: Chia-i, Hsin-chu, Chi-lung, T'ai-chung, T'ai-nan
Special municipalities: Kao-hsiung City, Taipei City

POPULATION
23,036,087 (July 2006 estimate)

LIFE EXPECTANCY
77.43 years (2006 estimate)

ETHNIC GROUPS
Taiwanese (including Hakka) 84 percent, mainland Chinese 14 percent, aborigines 2 percent.

RELIGIOUS GROUPS
Mixture of Buddhist, Confucian, and Taoist 93 percent, Christian 4.5 percent, other 2.5 percent.

LANGUAGES
Mandarin Chinese (official), Taiwanese (minority), Hakka dialects

TIME LINE

IN TAIWAN	IN THE WORLD
	753 B.C. Rome is founded. **116–17 B.C.** The Roman empire reaches its greatest extent, under Emperor Trajan (98–17).
A.D. 600 Island is occupied by aboriginal community of Austronesian descent.	**A.D. 600** Height of Mayan civilization **1000** The Chinese perfect gunpowder and begin to use it in warfare.
1517 Island is sighted by Portuguese vessels en route to Japan and named Ilha Formosa (which means Beautiful Island).	**1530** Beginning of transatlantic slave trade organized by the Portuguese in Africa. **1558–1603** Reign of Elizabeth I of England **1620** Pilgrims sail the *Mayflower* to America.
1624 Dutch occupy and control Formosa. **1662** Dutch are defeated by Chinese Ming general Cheng Cheng Kung (Koxinga) whose family rules Formosa for a short period. **1683** Annexed by China's rulers the Manchu Qing.	**1776** U.S. Declaration of Independence **1789–99** The French Revolution **1861** The U.S. Civil War begins. **1869** The Suez Canal is opened.
1895 Ceded "in perpetuity" to Japan under the Treaty of Shimonoseki at the end of the Sino-Japanese war. **1911** China becomes the Republic of China.	**1914** World War I begins.

IN TAIWAN	IN THE WORLD
	1939 World War II begins.
1945 Taiwan recovered by China's Nationalist Kuomintang government.	**1945** The United States drops atomic bombs on Hiroshima and Nagasaki.
1949 Flight of Nationalist government to Taiwan after Chinese Communist revolution. China becomes the People's Republic of China.	**1949** The North Atlantic Treaty Organization (NATO) is formed.
1954 United States–Taiwanese mutual defense treaty is signed.	**1957** The Russians launch Sputnik.
1971 Withdrawal from the UN as the United States adopts new policy of détente toward Communist China.	**1966–69** The Chinese Cultural Revolution
1986 Democratic Progressive Party (DPP) is formed as an opposition to nationalist Kuomintang (KMT).	**1986** Nuclear power disaster at Chernobyl in Ukraine **1991** Breakup of the Soviet Union **1997** Hong Kong is returned to China.
2000 Proindependence candidate, Chen Shui-bian, is elected president of Taiwan.	
2001 Taiwan partially lifts its 52-year ban on direct trade and communications with China.	**2001** Terrorists crash planes in New York, Washington, D.C., and Pennsylvania.
2002 Taiwan becomes a member of the WTO.	
2004 Chen Shui-bian is reelected as president of Taiwan, and the country's first national referendum is held.	**2003** War in Iraq
2005 An ad-hoc National Assembly was elected, symbolizing a major step forward for Taiwan's democratic reforms.	

GLOSSARY

cha (cha)
Tea, the national drink of Taiwan.

chang pao (CHAHNG pow)
Traditional costume for men.

chi pao (CHEE pow)
Traditional costume for women.

Confucianism
A code of conduct or value system that is a fundamental pillar of Chinese culture.

dim sum (DIM sum)
Cantonese-style snacks that are served with tea in Taiwan's tea houses. They are also known as *yum cha* (YAHM chah).

fan (fahn)
Rice, the staple food in Taiwan.

feng shui (FEHNG shway)
Literally meaning "wind and water," this oriental art of geomancy is based on the belief that non-living objects can influence people's living environment.

Han (Hahn)
The name given to the Chinese people who are believed to have originated from the central plains of China. Today the Han Chinese are the dominant ethnic group of China.

hsiao (SEE-ow)
The Confucian virtue of filial piety or respect and obedience to family elders.

kan pei (GAHN bay)
Literally meaning "bottoms up," it is like saying "cheers" during a toast.

Kuo yu (GWOH ewe-ee)
The national language, or Mandarin.

pinyin (PIN-yin)
The romanization system for the Chinese language that is used in mainland China.

shan (shahn)
Mountain.

tai chi chuan (TAI jee CHWAHN)
Also called tai chi, it is the Chinese art of shadow-boxing with meditative movements that is a popular leisure activity and form of exercise in Taiwan.

tai fong (TAI fohng)
Typhoon, or a tropical cyclone that commonly occurs in parts of Northeast Asia, especially in Taiwan, Hong Kong, and southern China.

Tongyong pinyin (TONG-yong Pin-yin)
System of writing Mandarin in English that has recently replaced the older system called Wade-Giles.

yuan (YOO-ahn)
Meaning "council." Taiwan's five *yuan* make up the national government, together with the president and National Assembly.

Yuanzhu min (YOO-AHN Ju min)
The Austronesian indigenous people of Taiwan.

FURTHER INFORMATION

BOOKS

Bender, Andrew, Julie Grundvig, and Robert Kelly. *Lonely Planet: Taiwan*. London: Lonely Planet Publications, 6th edition, 2004.

Li-Hung, Hsiao. Translated by Michelle Wu. *A Thousand Moons on a Thousand Rivers*. New York: Columbia University Press, 2000.

Roy, Denny. *Taiwan: A Political History*. Ithaca, NY: Cornell University Press, 2003.

"Taiwan." Economist Intelligence Unit Country Report (February 2006).

FILMS

City of Sadness. Directed by Hou Hsiao-hsien. 3-H Films, 1989.

Crouching Tiger, Hidden Dragon. Directed by Ang Lee. Sony Pictures Entertainment Inc., 2000.

Eat Drink Man Woman. Directed by Ang Lee. Samuel Goldwyn Company, 1994.

The Wedding Banquet. Directed by Ang Lee. Samuel Goldwyn Company, 1993.

WEB SITES

Asiaweek— Asia's best cities—Taipei. www.asiaweek.com/asiaweek/asiacities/taipei.html

China National Tourist Office. www.cnto.org/ac-history.asp

Department of Budget, Accounting and Statistics, Taipei City Government. http://english.taipei.gov.tw/dbas/index.jsp?categid=1334

Excite Travel. www.excite.co.uk/travel/guides/east_asia/taiwan/Currency

Taiwan Yearbook 2004. http://english.www.gov.tw/Yearbook/index.jsp

Taiwan Yearbook 2005. www.gio.gov.tw/taiwan-website/5-gp/yearbook/

The CIA World Factbook—Taiwan. www.cia.gov/cia/publications/factbook/geos/tw.html

The Taipei Times. www.taipeitimes.com/News/

The Tourist Bureau of Taiwan. www.taiwan.net.tw/lan/cht/index/index.asp

The 2-28 Massacre. http://228.lomaji.com/

Tiscali.reference—Taiwan. www.tiscali.co.uk/reference/encyclopaedia/countryfacts/taiwan.html

BIBLIOGRAPHY

Cromie, Alice. *Taiwan*. Chicago, IL: Children's Press, 1994.

Harmon, Tim D. *The Land and People: The Republic of China*. Hillsboro, OR: Beyond Words Publications, 1992.

Mackay, George L. *From Far Formosa: The Island, Its People and Missions*. Edinburgh: Oliphant Anderson and Ferrier, 1896.

Rubinstein, Murray (editor). *The Other Taiwan: 1945 to the Present*. New York: M. E. Sharpe, 1994.

Yu, Ling, and Jon A Teta. *Taiwan in Pictures*. Minneapolis, MN: Lerner Publications, 1989.

INDEX